CHAPTER O

Robert Evans had never hit a cricket ball as hard. The loud thwack as the willow met the leather was in direct contrast to the peaceful atmosphere of the little cricket ground nestled in had ruffled the peace of the sylvan surroundings – the umpire calling" over" or the occasional more raucous "well bowled" as the quick bowlers tested the mettle of the openers. Robert and his fellow opener Brian Morgan had amassed twenty runs thus far, by means of gentle nudges, delicate cuts, and the occasional classic cover drive, stroked rather than hit aggressively. The three elderly spectators had settled comfortably into their deck chairs, basking in the warm summer sun in the July of 1946, and looking forward to an afternoon of free entertainment. It was always a question of which of them would fall asleep first, and who would snore the loudest. They had all been cricketers in their time, and undoubtedly dreamed of past heroic innings they had played, or hat-tricks they had achieved, all clean bowled of course.

Robert had faced this fast bowler many times before. They knew each other well, Robert as the village bobby, and Ian Friend as the local tearaway. The cricket field offered the one place where Ian could legally confront the law on level terms. His latest escapade had been where Robert had caught him riding his old motorbike on the pavement, terrifying old ladies doing their shopping in the little shops in the village. A fine had resulted and Ian's hatred of the copper had grown with each day which passed. Today he resolved to bowl as fast as possible against this man who he regarded as his enemy .Robert was ready for this torrent of very rapid deliveries and had managed to survive with some difficulty, scoring only the odd single from Ian's bowling. He could see that Ian was really fired up for the contest today, and that getting runs would not come easily. However he was surprised and angered when the fast bowler let loose a bouncer which flicked Robert's cap before racing away to the boundary over the wicket keeper's head. All were shocked at this vicious delivery for bouncers were strictly forbidden at this level of cricket.

As the umpire wagged his finger at the bowler and Ian's captain admonished him with "that's enough of that my lad," Robert, seething inside, strolled down the pitch, stony-faced, and controlling his emotions, patted the ground right at the bowler's feet, while looking him in the eye with disgust. They stood for some seconds glaring at each other, until Brian pulled his fellow batsman away and led him back to his own crease. The only satisfactory outcome of that unsavoury incident was that the umpire had credited Robert with four runs from the headed boundary. Still angry, he disciplined himself to face up to the next ball. When it arrived it was a slower juicy half-volley.

Robert, naturally known to all of his friends as Bob, was a big man, some six foot three tall, with broad shoulders, and burly as befits a village bobby. He was twenty six years old, married with a pretty little three year old daughter Emily, on whom he doted. His wife, Anne was the same age as her husband. She was slim, fair haired with an engaging smile. She did playground duties at the local village school, and was currently studying with a view to eventually becoming a teacher. Both Robert and Anne were local people, and had met as pupils at the little school, before going to the senior school in the nearby town where their romance had really begun. Their relationship was readily approved by both their families, and their decision to marry in 1940 was greatly welcomed by all. After a brief honeymoon spent in an old thatched hotel on Dartmoor, Robert enlisted in the army where he trained as a radio man. He served in North Africa with the desert rats, and later in Italy where he was injured by shrapnel when a mortar shell landed near him. Shipped back to England, he spent some weeks recuperating, and, when the war in Europe ended, was demobbed and able to return to civilian life. On one of the few leaves he had spent with Anne, little Emily was conceived. She was born in 1943and christened in the local church of St. Michael.

Robert had worked conscientiously at school and, when he left he was taken on as a solicitor's clerk. Although he was happy to be earning quite good money in a friendly environment, and was able to spend more time with Anne and little Emily, he longed for a more active lifestyle. Attending court one day a police inspector, giving evidence in a case of larceny, approached Robert and invited him to join him for tea in the canteen. The inspector, Harold Pengelly, had only recently joined the local force. Little was known of him, but he had produced all of the right credentials, and was proving himself to be a competent officer. Robert had spoken at length with Anne and with his parents, and decided that the work of a police officer would give him more variety in his life, and would be healthier than sitting in an office, interesting though that work often was. It was in that solicitor's workplace that he had first heard the name of the fired-up fast bowler who had just attempted to remove his head from his shoulders with that wicked short ball.

It was the summer of 1946. Although the war had been over for some months now, the after effects were still being felt, especially by those who had lost loved ones during that dreadful conflict. The village, tucked away in the countryside, had not suffered the agony of bombing which had afflicted the cities and military establishments like the nearby airfields. Towards the end of the hostilities doodlebugs, Hitler's revenge weapons, had, for a brief period brought terror to the people. One had crashed on the outskirts of the village causing much damage, but fortunately inflicting no casualties. Life was slowly returning to the normality of pre-war Britain, though rationing was a burden which threatened to last for some time.

Now he was a fully trained village bobby, respected by almost everybody on his quite extensive patch which took in three smallish villages, some scattered farms with their associated labourers' cottages, and much woodland and fields where cereals grew, and grass meadows on which cattle and sheep grazed. Generally for Robert, and indeed for the community it was a peaceful existence. The weekly cricket match usually mirrored that tranquillity, and unleashing a bouncer was certainly not the done thing. The game was a local derby against the nearby village of Hawksmead a community which was also Robert's responsibility. The two hamlets were roughly equal in size, the inhabitants mostly involved in agriculture, with just a few commuting daily to the nearby town on their bicycles. The two villages were situated along a pretty valley, some three miles apart. Through both hamlets meandered a gentle stream, which, in the wet months, could sometimes cause flooding to those houses on its banks.

CHAPTER TWO

As he faced up to the next delivery Robert was angry, but it was a controlled anger, knowing that he must keep calm. His wartime experiences had taught him the futility of losing his nerve. What if Friend, ignoring the hostility he was receiving, even from some of his own side, decided to bowl yet another bouncer at him? He squared his broad shoulders and faced the bowler, a look of determination on his face. Maybe a little shamefaced at the reception his previous delivery had received, the next ball was considerably slower, and well-pitched up. It was a ball every opening batsman would relish, a juicy half-volley. One pace forward and a full swing of the bat with all the power of his muscular shoulders, and his pent up anger behind it, Robert, head down over the shot, caught the red ball right in the middle of the bat, and watched as it soared off over the bowler's head towards the long-off boundary. It never achieved a great height, but followed a flat trajectory to clear the fence at the bottom of the field and continue towards the stand of trees on the other side of the little lane which weaved its carefree way past the cricket ground. Everyone, players, umpires, scorers, and even the three elderly spectators, awakened by the violent sound of bat on ball, watched as the ball disappeared from view and vanished from sight into the trees. A smattering of applause came from the pavilion where Robert's teammates were sitting awaiting their turn to go in to bat. One of the trio of spectators turned to his companions and muttered begrudgingly "Not a bad shot, but I've seen better."

In the nets were some young lads, whose dads were playing in the match. On hearing the mighty crack of bat on willow they had stopped practising to see the ball fly into the wood. Instinctively they raced towards where they thought the ball had landed hoping to retrieve it. Leaping over the stile at the back of the pavilion, they scampered along the lane until a break in the hedge gave them access to the wood. They then vanished from sight. On the field most of the fielders lay down welcoming the rest, and enjoying the warmth of the sun. The two umpires came together examining the spare ball they carried, choosing which one they would select should the trees not produce the match ball. Brian walked down the pitch to Robert and, clapping his friend on the shoulder exclaimed "That was a great shot Rob". Ian scowled and kicked the turf in frustration. He came from Hawksmead, and the rivalry between the two villages had continued for decades, always fiercely fought but with mutual respect between the players.

The two batsmen looked at the scoreboard and discussed the situation. Although they were going well they knew that a big score would be essential today as the opposition had some formidable, hard-hitting batsmen. Brian wondered if Ian's skipper would now take him off and condemn him to the far reaches of the outfield where he could sulk alone. Their musings were rudely interrupted by a hysterical cry emanating from the wood. All eyes turned towards the sound, only to see one of the boys burst through the hedge, closely followed by his companions. All were now shouting while pointing towards the wood behind them. The fielder nearest to them, at long on, strolled casually to the boundary telling the lads to calm down and tell what had so excited them. "There's a body in there" stuttered the largest of the boys "It's a lady, and she looks dead" said his friend, tears beginning to roll down his ruddy cheeks. The wood was called Minnis Wood, and the lane which rolled by it was too named Minnis. It was not an extensive stand of trees, and consisted of mainly beech and oak with a smattering of fir trees. It was a part of Dave Chalmers' farm, and he had no idea how the wood had got its name.

All of the participants in the match, fielders, batsmen, and umpires walked, some purposefully, some a little apprehensively to the clearly upset boys. Even the three deckchair users looked bemusedly at the sight of all of the cricketers, apparently leaving the field of action. "Is that it then?" said one "And we haven't had our tea yet!" As the representative of the law Robert knew that it was his duty to find out what had so disturbed the young boys, and, despite being hampered by his pads was the first to reach the fence, and to enter the lane where the lads were standing, hopping from foot to foot. The other players remained on the field, standing at the boundary fence, leaving it to the policeman to find out what had happened. The big lad, Jimmy, repeated what he had said "There's a dead lady in there sir, I think you've killed her with that six you just hit."

Handing his bat to Jimmy, and telling the boys to stay in the lane, Robert proceeded to push through the gap in the hedge and forced his way through the bushes and brambles in the direction indicated by the frightened Jimmy. Some twenty yards into the trees he found a body, clearly a woman, lying face down on the ground, her head just touching a huge beech tree, a mute witness to what was obviously a tragic death. He felt for a pulse, noting that, despite the warmth of the day, the body was cold. She had been dead for some time, and he was relieved that he had certainly not been responsible for her death. His police training now took control. He walked back to the lane, and confirmed to the cricketers what the boys had said. He thanked the lads for their actions and told them to go back to the pavilion, saying that he would need to speak to them later. He then asked Brian to run to the village to call the police from the phone box outside the newsagent's shop. Robert then told the captain of the fielding side that he would, of course, have to retire, but asked him if they wanted to carry on with the match. After some discussion, and talking to the batting side who had come from the pavilion to see what was happening, the general consensus was for carrying on since the place where the "accident" had occurred was not on the cricket field. Robert warned them that they would all be interviewed by CID officers before being allowed to leave the ground. "I suppose they'll blame me as usual" growled Ian, and he lurched off, a thoroughly disgruntled young man.

As the players drifted off to resume the cricket match, and Robert's replacement batsman came to the wicket, Brian raced back from his trip to the phone box, and took his place at the crease. Robert now retraced his steps to the body in the wood. Examining the corpse he could see that it was, as he had first thought, that of a woman. Without seeing her face which was pressed to the ground, he had the distinct impression that it was a tall youngish woman lying there on her front. She had short black hair, slightly dishevelled, with greeny –brown trousers, and was barefooted. He looked for signs of the cricket ball hitting her, but knew that he would find none. Maybe when the forensic people turned her over they would discover a bruise or other injury on her face. Without wanting to disturb the scene he looked around to see if he could find the ball which he had so violently hit in this direction.

As he stood there looking down at the pitiable body which had once been a vital human being, he felt sick and at the same time mystified at her death. As a soldier he had become used to seeing people killed, but this had not happened on the battlefield, but in the peaceful surroundings of the English countryside on a warm summer's day where violence was the last thing to be expected. His policeman's instinct cut in and he looked round, without moving, careful not to disturb the scene, for signs indicating how the young woman had come to be there. He knew everyone in the villages for which he was responsible, and didn't think he could recognise the young lady lying lifeless at his feet.

Some twenty minutes later he heard the welcome sound of the police vehicles rushing to the scene, their bells disturbing the peace of the countryside. He walked to the lane and stood waiting for his colleagues to arrive. He was relieved to see Inspector Pengelly step out of the first car, followed by the forensic expert Doctor Buchanan, affectionately known as the Prof. As his name suggested the doctor was Scottish, who, when excited, spoke with an accent that no-one could decipher. On leaving the car, he looked around, and, on seeing the cricketers, all immaculately dressed in their whites, proclaimed loudly "Game for sissies!" He said this with a broad grin on his ruddy face, knowing that no offence would be taken. He now turned his corpulent body towards Robert and said "now Robbie what have you got for me today?" Despite the seriousness of the situation Robert could not suppress a smile as the doctor gripped his hand with his enormous paw. Compared with the smartly dressed cricketers, and the uniformed policemen, the prof was the epitome of scruffiness. As ever he was sporting a dirty green smock with matching green calf length boots. On his head was a flat cap, green of course, which had clearly seen better days and an unruly grey beard, through which protruded a beak of a nose on which rested perfectly round horn-rimmed glasses.

Though his appearance was somewhat bizarre, no-one took him for a fool. He was a renowned pathologist, and had been involved in many famous cases. The sparkling blue eyes concealed a brilliant mind, and his evidence had brought some notable criminals to book. As he prepared to follow Robert in to the wood he called to one of the constables standing by the police car "My bag laddie, if you please" and fought his way through the bushes, not brushing them aside but barging through them. Inspector Pengelly too entered the wood, ordering the constables to remain in the lane and to block both ends of it. On the field, near the boundary, Ian Friend could not stop himself from calling out "Never seen so many coppers in one place in my life!"

The prof stood for some long moments examining the body on the ground. He then gently turned it over, and once again stood looking at her, deep in thought. Robert and the inspector too looked at the lifeless young girl, noting how pretty she was, and how young she actually was. White faced, her wide open brown eyes displayed a look of terror. As he looked down Robert had a feeling of great relief as he saw the wide bloodstain which covered her chest. It was confirmed that his mighty six hit had not killed this person, she had almost certainly been murdered. At this stage the doctor's examination of the corpse was purely a visual one. After some consideration he turned to the inspector and to Robert and declaimed "Looks like a knife wound to the heart, death would have been instantaneous, and she was probably killed here. As to time of death, I should say, without a detailed examination, last night, maybe around midnight". Staring intently for a short while longer, he turned on his heel, and, telling the inspector that he would give a detailed analysis of the cause of death when he had taken the body to his lab, he stumbled off to the lane. As he negotiated the brambles and bushes a robin flew overhead as though it was guiding the portly gentleman to safety. With redbreast belligerently pushed forward, it berated these noisy intruders with a shrill whistle. The prof pointed to the offending bird and said to the officers in the road "There's your witness, take its name!", "Sure it's not the killer prof?" retorted one of the men, grinning at the venerable scientist.

Telling Robert to stay by the victim while he organised a search of the wood, and the fields around it, the inspector too negotiated the bushes to reach the lane where his men awaited orders. Robert now knelt down to examine the features of the girl more closely. He knew everybody in the communities he served, and could not recognise this young lady. Could she be a relative of one of the villagers, or maybe someone just visiting? For him crime here in this quiet corner of the country consisted of motoring offences, the occasional vandalism, just one burglary (as yet unsolved), and the inevitable poaching. At that thought he felt a twinge of conscience as he, in his youth, had not been averse to bagging the odd rabbit or pheasant. Fortunately he had never been caught!

An ambulance had now arrived, and a pair of stretcher bearers, under the careful supervision of Inspector Pengelly, carefully picked up the pathetic bundle and made their tortuous way to their vehicle. Their precious cargo safely installed inside, the ambulance set off for the local hospital and its laboratory where the doctor could do his work. With all of this activity going on it was almost impossible for the cricketers to concentrate on the game. The fielding became sloppy, catches were dropped, and batsmen got out to shots they would normally not play. Ian was not asked to bowl any more, and was banished to the outfield.

CHAPTER THREE

Robert walked slowly back along the lane to the pavilion where his fellow team-mates were eager to question him about the non-cricket activity which was taking place, distracting them from the really important business of beating the opposition. He told them of finding the body of the dead young lady in the wood, and how, at first, he thought he may have killed her with the ball he had hit so hard into the trees. As he was explaining this one of the police officers entered the pavilion, and began taking names and addresses, so that they could be interviewed later. Turning to Robert he handed him the ball which had been found by the men meticulously searching the scene. The ball was still shiny red, and unmarked. He now realised that he was still wearing his batting pads and his box, so he quickly removed them, and gratefully accepted a hot cup of tea brought to him by one of the ladies who prepared the refreshments for the players between innings. He asked one of the lads to go and tell Anne, his wife that he was alright, and that he would tell her later about the excitement at the match. He knew that she, together with the other villagers, would be concerned about the police activity and would wonder what had happened.

Teatime arrived and the players trooped off the field, discussing, not the state of the match, but the extraordinary events which Robert's hard hit boundary had triggered. More police arrived to talk to everyone in the pavilion, including the refreshment ladies and the three elderly spectators, who were having a really fascinating day. For these worthy gentlemen this was the most exciting thing which had happened since a stray doodlebug had plummeted to earth near St Michaels Church early one morning awakening everybody, bar the vicar, and damaging many buildings. Fortunately there were no casualties except a few hens, who emerged from their house, cackling away and with some feathers missing. For a few days egg-laying was not as productive as usual.

Over tea and the inevitable cucumber sandwiches, followed by the usual delicious home-made cakes, Robert's captain talked about the state of the game and what the men thought they should do in view of the tragedy which had occurred. In terms of pure figures the team had not done well. Despite a valiant half-century from Brian a paltry total of only 150 runs had been recorded. The skipper felt that, in fairness to the opposition, he should declare the innings closed now. The consensus was to discuss the situation with the other team to see if they wanted to carry on with the match. Players of both teams, together with the two umpires and the scorers, gathered together on the veranda of the pavilion, and all were asked what they wanted to do. To the disappointment of the trio of deckchair spectators, the decision was made to abandon the game to show respect to the deceased young lady in the copse. Ian Friend's was the only dissenting voice, and, without bidding farewell he mounted his bike and drove furiously off to the Kings Arms pub.

Now the landlord of the said hostelry Stan, was the father of one of Robert's team-mates. He welcomed the influx of customers from the now abandoned cricket match, as the vast majority of the participants in that unfortunate contest entered his premises in the age old tradition of ending a good old game of cricket with a pint or two of good old English ale. Today, of course, the talk was not of glorious batting, bowling or fielding, or even of dodgy umpiring decisions, but of the strange and disturbing happenings among the trees. Ian, with a head start on the quaffing of beer, asserted, looking at Robert, "You can't blame me this time, I was on the field with all of you". "But we don't know when the girl was killed do we, and it was only your crap bowling which led to the discovery of the body". This from Robert's captain. Robert now felt the need to enter into the conversation, and, without trying to exercise his authority as a law officer, gently explained that speculation was a pointless exercise, and that we all needed to see what the police investigation would uncover. At that the talk turned to the game of cricket, the test matches being played, and the next games to be played by the two village teams.

The wives of the players, and other villagers hurried to the Kings Arms, the news of the tragedy in the wood having quickly spread, as is ever the case in all small communities. The pub soon filled up, and the landlord's till was extremely busy, as all of the chat about the events of the day made for thirsty customers. For landlord Stan it was like Christmas in the middle of summer! As more and more pints were supped the noise level in the small pub grew ever louder, and conclusions as to what had actually occurred became ever more outrageous. However the atmosphere remained convivial, until Ian, now well into his cups began to argue in his usual belligerent manner with one of Robert's teammates. Fortunately Ian's captain managed to calm him down which saved Robert having to intervene.

CHAPTER FOUR

Anne opened the door of their little cottage when she saw her husband at the gate. She had heard of the death of the young lady, and noticed the distracted look on Robert's face. She greeted him with a hug and kiss, and called to little Emily, busily playing with her toys. On hearing her dad's voice she ran to him and covered his face with sloppy kisses. The warm welcome from his family helped him to put the disturbing events of the afternoon to the back of his mind, and he took his daughter to the lawn at the rear of the house, and, placing her on the swing, proceeded to induce squeals of delight from her as he swung her higher and higher. Awoken from her afternoon nap, Emily's little black and white springer spaniel scampered to join them, racing around, tail wagging, and yelping happily.

It was later that evening, Emily now fast asleep, after listening to her dad reading to her about beautiful princesses and handsome princes, and the puppy, Meg, curled up on her rug beside her bed. Robert and Anne sat close together on the veranda, and Robert told his wife all about the tragedy in the wood, and how, at first, it was feared that he had been responsible for the death. He asked his wife if she knew of any new people moving in to the area recently, saying that he could not identify the girl. Anne shook her head, saying that the only movement had been that of a family leaving the village to join relatives in London. She said that, with the war finished, the few evacuees from the cities had returned home, and there were no strangers in the village as far as she knew.

Sleep did not come easily to Robert that night. He could not rid his mind of the sight of that poor young woman lying lifelessly on the ground under the trees. He could not help but speculate how she had arrived at that spot, and how terrified she must have been before being brutally murdered. He resolved to track down the assassin and bring him before the law.

He was awake early the next bright sunny morning. Carefully so as not to disturb Anne, he tiptoed out of the bedroom, and quietly opened the door of his daughter's room. Emily was still fast asleep, as was Meg, now on the bed, snuggled up to his daughter. He stood for some time regarding the peaceful scene, and thought how fortunate he was to have such a loving family. In the kitchen, as he waited for the kettle to boil for his first cup of tea of the day, the door was pushed gently open and Meg waddled in, tail wagging furiously as ever. He let the little black and white dog out into the garden, and stood for a moment breathing in the warm, scented air. The huge yellow sun was now appearing over the trees, promising yet another glorious day. There was barely a breath of wind, and the only sounds were the hedge sparrows twittering away, bidding their own welcome to the newly born day.

The little cottage was built on a hill overlooking the village of Elwood, a community nestled in the green countryside of the garden of England. It was in this hamlet that both Robert and his wife had been born, as had their parents before them. Indeed Anne had barely left the village, attending school there, working there, and only venturing out to the nearby town for shopping, and the occasional visit to the cinema. Any chance of a holiday had been stolen at the advent of war, and trips to the seaside were now a distant memory. However she was very content with her lot, successful at school, a long courtship with Robert, always fit and healthy, with her parents still close by, and many friends in the village. She, and her husband to be were members of the choir in the village church. It was in that church, St. Michaels that they had been married and their Emily had been christened there. Anne and her husband were well thought of, respected members of the community.

As he stood there in his garden Robert mused how good life was for him and his family. He smiled as he thought of their wedding day, and the cricketers with bats raised providing a guard of honour. The war had obviously not been a pleasant experience for him, but he felt that, being away from his home, and seeing different parts of the world, had given him a wider perspective on life .As he looked down over the village, seeing the tree-lined lanes and avenues, the stream which meandered gently through it on its casual way to the sea, and the church spire rising to the blue sky, and dreaming in the strong sunlight, he knew that he would not willingly give up all of this easily. Beyond the village he could see the stands of beech and oak trees climbing up the slopes towards the summit of the towering Oak Hill. On the flatlands beneath the trees sheep grazed contentedly, their growing lambs gambolling around them. A flock of rooks majestically flew over the church seeking their feeding grounds for today. To his left Robert could see farmer Dave Chalmers' Friesian cows making their languid way to the milking shed. Now the church bell sonorously rang out to chime six o'clock, and Robert called Meg back into the house, where he sat down, with tea in hand to hear the news broadcast on the radio.

It now being Sunday, Robert would not normally be going out on patrol today, but, in view of the events of the previous day, he felt that he ought to call the local police station to see if he would be needed. The sergeant assured him that he could stay at home with his family, but that, if he were needed, he would be contacted. Emily now entered the kitchen and, rubbing the sleep from her eyes, climbed on to her dad's lap, sat there, blissfully sucking her thumb. Anne now appeared, hugged them both, and began to prepare breakfast for them all. Robert explained that they could spend the day as they liked as the station did not need him to work today but that he might receive a call later.

They sat in the garden in the shade of the conker tree which bordered their property. Emily eagerly tucked into her puffed wheat, while the adults enjoyed a cooked breakfast of bacon, eggs and toast. Anne asked their daughter what she would like to do today. In her piping voice she shouted "The stream mummy please." For the little girl it was always the little river, and, the dishes washed, and the kitchen tidy, the Evans family set off for the village and the stream, Emily perched precariously on her dads' shoulder. They strolled down the lane, passing little groups of people, standing by their garden gates, deep in conversation, inevitably about the strange cricket match. They bid cheerful greetings to the Evans, but fortunately refrained from asking Robert if there was any more news. At the door of St Michaels church the Reverend Harris stood greeting the worshippers waiting to enter the church for morning service. He bade good morning to Robert and Anne and fondly tickled Emily's chin.

Finally they reached the watercourse and the old stone bridge which crossed it. Eagerly Emily, now back on the ground, ran to the parapet of the bridge and looked excitedly down at the slow moving current to see if she could see the many little fishes which lived there. Anne held firmly on to her daughter to make certain that she didn't topple over and join the trout and grayling gracefully swimming by. The water was so clear that the images of the few passing clouds were reflected in it. Spellbound the little girl peered down at the shimmering current, and squealing, pointed to each fish as it lazily swam under the bridge. Now she would run to and fro to mark the progress of each swimmer, her little face lit up with sheer joy and wonder. Dad had fetched some twigs and they could all play the game of seeing whose stick, when thrown in, passed under the bridge first. Emily, of course, always claimed victory.

They finally managed to drag their daughter away from the water, promising that they would come back again soon. Walking through the village once again, Emily now insisting on walking, at least for a part of the way, they stopped at the newsagent's shop to buy ice creams and a Sunday newspaper. Then it was back home to be greeted by a miserable Meg, sulking because she had not been allowed to join the family at the river. She had gone with them once but had disgraced herself by falling in the water, and, on emerging had sprayed everyone with water as she shook herself vigorously. The remainder of that Sunday was spent largely relaxing. After a most satisfying lunch, eaten outside to take advantage of the beautiful weather, Emily fell asleep, worn out by the adventures of the day. Anne and Robert sat together on the garden bench, occasionally chatting in a desultory manner, but largely drinking in the peace and beauty of their surroundings. With the sun beaming down the buildings of the village had never looked more sublime, cottages, houses, farm houses and barns and sheds, and particularly the old church, with its thirteenth century spire reaching high up into the sky as if in tribute to the great yellow orb which warmed and gave it a pearly glow. Anne recalled that it was just such a day when she and Robert had exchanged rings in the same church, and she squeezed her husband's hand at the memory. Both of them realised how fortunate they were to live in such a beautiful part of the country, a country now at peace after the trauma of the recent war. But for Robert he still could not shake off the vision of the corpse in the wood.

Meg was fussing around and Robert set off to take the little dog for her daily walk. Without thinking his steps were guided to the cricket field, now deserted as was the pavilion. He walked to the wicket and stood where he had taken guard only yesterday. He went through the events of the afternoon, the bouncer from Ian, and the tremendous six he had hit clearing the far boundary. He looked at the lane which wound up the slope in the direction of the next village. Beyond the trees he knew was Dave Chalmers' farm, with the field immediately beyond the trees was a grass meadow ready for a second cut of hay. Further on up the valley he could see the huts of the prisoner of war's camp for soldiers awaiting repatriation. It was a part of his duties to visit it once a week to check with the guards at the gate, and he was largely well received there. While serving in Italy he had picked up a smattering of the language, and was able to have simple disjointed conversations with the Italian detainees who would come to the gate to see him. They were fairly loosely guarded, and not considered a threat to the country now that the war was over. Some worked on local farms where their help was gratefully received. One of the detainees, a young soldier named Luigi, had carved a little dog for Emily, and it was her pride and joy. For some perverse reason she had named it Knees. When asked why she replied "Because that's her name".

While Robert stood deep in thought, Meg was racing around in the wood, hunting for her favourite prey – rabbits. Having failed to find any she scampered out of the trees and came to her master, as usual bits of bramble sticking to her fur. Robert tidied her up and the twosome set off for home again.

CHAPTER FIVE

He slept more deeply that night, and awoke the next morning refreshed, and ready to face whatever the day might bring. After breakfast he put on his police uniform, and prepared to follow his usual routine. This would involve patrolling his rather large beat on his motorcycle, and dealing with any problems which might arise. He always varied his route so that any would-be villains might be caught out by his unexpected appearance. However today was to be different as he received a call from the station telling him to report immediately. This was a rather peremptory summons, out of tune with the casual tenor of life here deep in the English countryside.

It was a pleasant half hour ride to the police station in the centre of the town. There was very little traffic at that time of the morning, just the occasional milkman, the postman and the tanker lorry collecting milk from the dairy farms. He parked his motor bike outside the station and went in to be greeted by Inspector Pengelly. "Come on Robert, "he said, "We're off to see the prof, he's got something to tell us". The two got in a police car and set off for the forensic lab, which was attached to the local university. On the way the inspector said that there was something odd about this murder, and we're going to have to rely on your local knowledge if we're to solve it. Intrigued Robert could not wait to see the old prof and to discover the "something odd" about the case.

Doctor Buchanan was his usual ebullient self, and he greeted the two policemen with his customary warmth. Clad in a voluminous green apron which almost reached the floor, and today sporting a tartan beret, he led them in to the mortuary where, lying on a steel table in the middle of the room, was the body of the young lady from the wood. There were clear signs that he prof had carried out a post mortem, and the officers were both disturbed at the sight. They could see that she had been a very pretty, well-made woman, slim and fit looking. The prof pointed to the knife wound in the chest. "Six inch blade with a serrated edge" he said. "Straight to the heart with a downward stroke. Death would have been instantaneous". He now pointed to her arms which were smooth with no signs of defensive wounds. "She was not interfered with sexually either" he added. Gently turning the body with his huge hands he said "Now for the strange bit, for which I have no explanation at present".

Across the top of the shoulders was a livid red scar as though something very hot had been applied to the skin. It was about three inches long and one inch wide, and looked as though attempts had been made to disguise a tattoo of some sort. Only the first letter, symbol or number had not been completely eliminated. The prof said "We've looked at it through the microscope and it looks like a "c", and, judging by the size of the letter perhaps some three, or maybe four other symbols have been obliterated. It looks as though the burning was done fairly recently, perhaps only a short time before her death. Incidentally I calculate that she was killed sometime on Friday night, perhaps between midnight and two am." The inspector cut in to say that she had probably died on the spot where she was found as no drag marks had been found after a pretty exhaustive search of the wood had been carried out. The prof then said that he would get some of his minions to conduct a more detailed forensic examination of the area to see if any clues of any sort could be found.

As the officers left the mortuary, pondering the mystery of the "c" on the girl's back, the inspector said to Robert that he would be relying on him to think carefully about the inhabitants of his two villagers, to note if anyone had changed their daily routine of late. The participants in the cricket match would now be questioned once again now that the time of death had been established. He also asked Robert to call meetings in the villages to ask for information and to assure the people of their safety. More patrol cars would be deployed for a while to re-assure everybody. He asked Robert to report daily on anything which might help to solve the murder. He also told him that there should be no mention of the strange scarring on the victim's back as it might lead to all sorts of fanciful theories.

He followed his customary beat on his way home for lunch and as he passed each dwelling he thought of the inhabitants therein trying to think who might be a murderer, and who would burn the skin of a young lady in such a horrendous and painful way. He rapidly came to the conclusion that nobody of his acquaintance would be capable of such a dastardly deed. The only violence he had been called on to deal with had been when the pubs closed at night and alcohol caused some people, usually young men, to act in an irrational manner. The only really oddball character in Elwood was Silly Bill, an ex-soldier shell-shocked from the First World War. He was to be seen every day, regardless of the weather, atop his old bicycle riding along the lanes and footpaths, and even through the woods. Nobody minded that he was poacher, and a very skilled one, selling his rabbits to the local butcher. A tall, slim scruffily dressed man, he was harmless, and accepted by all. He lived with his sister Liz in a little cottage near the church, and was employed by the vicar to keep the graveyard tidy. He could often be seen with his old scythe cutting the grass between the graves. He rarely spoke, and, when the boys asked him the time it was always "Ten past two". Only he knew the significance of this particular time, but it clearly related to some traumatic incident which had occurred in the trenches. Robert knew that Bill's knowledge of the district was greater even than his, and indeed he had seen the old soldier cycling through the very wood where the body had been found. However there would be no point in questioning him, and it might even upset him.

Robert decided to visit Dave Chalmers on whose land stood the wood which was the scene of the murder. This farm was, by a distance the largest in the area. It was good fertile arable land, year on year producing huge yields of wheat, barley and potatoes. The grass meadows produced copious amounts of hay for the cattle, sheep and horses during the winter months. On his off days Robert loved to help out, and Anne too was ever eager to be with the animals. She especially liked lambing time and would take little Emily to help feeding the few motherless lambs with bottles of milk. Anne could also turn her hand at milking the herd of Friesian cattle, and Dave was more than happy to let her and Robert milk his cows. Emily would sit and watch her parents as they went from cow to cow, and she knew all of their names. In her piping voice she would call out "Daphne's next mum, and don't forget Daisy."

Dave was tinkering with his Fordson tractor when Robert arrived. A rather short, burly man, red of face, sporting as ever a rather mucky overall, boots and a flat cap of an indeterminate colour. Greeting him Robert thought "this man could only be a farmer". "Bloody machine" complained Dave "don't want to start, I've spoken nicely to it, even kicked it, but it won't fire up. Horses were a lot less trouble you know Robert." The policeman smiled and began the procedure needed to persuade the tractor to burst into life. Checking the petrol, he adjusted the choke and throttle, then went round to the front where he vigorously swung the starting handle. After two turns the machine gloriously started up, shattering the peace and quiet of the farmyard. The two men smiled at each other, and Dave grasped Robert's hand in thanks.

It was the farmer who brought up the subject of the death in the wood. This was inevitable since he owned that particular piece of land. When told that the death had occurred on Friday night, he mused for a moment and then said that he had noticed nothing unusual during that day. He had walked the meadow adjoining the wood during the morning, checking on his ewes and lambs, and all appeared to be normal. He said that, as usual, there were some young lads playing among the trees, and they had happily called out to him as he walked by. Smiling broadly, and grabbing Robert's arm he went on to say that, come the evening there would be some older youngsters playing slightly different games! "Maybe you'd like to talk to them to see if they had seen anything out of the ordinary. We both know who these young folk are don't we?" Robert thanked him and said that he would make discrete enquiries, without telling their parents why he was questioning their little darlings.

The conversation now turned to the farm itself. Dave said that he was having a good year, a better than average lambing, and the wheat and barley looking promising. Robert knew that they had harvested a healthy crop of hay, as he had helped with the hay-making. The cows were all well, and calving had been achieved without any problems- no vet bills he grinned. Robert asked him about the extensive woodland which abutted Dave's farm. He knew that he had sold the some fifty acres of woodland to some consortium, and had made good money from the sale. He knew nothing of the new owners, and indeed had never seen them, the transaction being done by lawyers in London. They both looked towards the impressive stand of trees which dominated the landscape, being on a steep slope behind which the bright sun shone casting deep shadows across the field of growing wheat on Dave's farm. "They've installed a pretty hefty fence round the trees, maybe they're frightened about trespassers, or even poachers". They both thought immediately of Ian Friend, the demon fast bowler and prolific trapper of rabbits and other animals and birds.

"Before I sold the land, we used to rear a few pheasants there, and, in the shooting season, I'd invite some friends to a day's sport in the trees, taking the odd pheasant, woodcock, and, of course a pigeon or two. There used to be several badger's setts in there, a fox or two as well I shouldn't wonder. But what goes on in there now is a bit of a mystery to me. When I've walked along the fence by the wood I've sometimes heard voices, and noticed movement, but I've never actually seen anyone in there." At regular intervals along the fence were notices held up on tall posts. Robert asked what they were for, as they were too far away for him to be able to read. "Keep out .Trespassers will be prosecuted" said Dave. "Must be something important in there, or some secret us peasants are not allowed to see. It doesn't really concern me, and it doesn't interfere with my business. Nonetheless I do wonder what the new owners intend to do with the wood. I just hope they never decide to fell all those beautiful trees.

Scanning the forest from left to right, Robert felt there was something intimidating about it as it climbed up the steep slope casting deep shadows over the meadow below it. The trees were mostly magnificent, towering beech with their grey/green trunks, and beautiful foliage. However there were also some equally tall conifers, and it was these dark evergreens which gave the wood an aura of mystery, almost of menace. He resolved to make enquiries about the wood, and its owners, and maybe request their permission to walk through it since it actually came within his area of responsibility. He might even talk to Ian Friend to see what he knew about the forest, but whether he would co-operate might be a problem. He also thought that it was a near certainty that old Bill had penetrated the fences to explore within, even if it meant leaving his bike outside the wood.

CHAPTER SIX

Robert bade the farmer goodbye, promising to help out with the milking at the weekend. He said that detectives would undoubtedly be coming to question him about the murder, and Dave said that he was expecting that. Now home to lunch, to take refreshments and to write up his report on the morning's happenings. He told Anne about his visit to the farm, and asked her if she had heard any talk about the dark brooding wood. She shook her head, and then asked about the tattoo on the girl's back. He described it to her and said that, at the moment they had no idea what it meant. Anne was appalled thinking of the agony the girl must have experienced when the heat was applied to her skin. Looking at her husband she muttered "Who could do something like that to another human being?" She then considered for a moment and speculated "Could the "c" be short for a name like Carol? Or maybe the start of a number using roman numerals, you know "c" meaning a hundred?" Robert replied that they were only guessing at the moment, but that more experts were at this moment examining the awful scar to see if any sense could be made of it. So far no-one had come up with a plausible explanation.

Saying a fond farewell to Anne, Emily and Meg, Robert mounted his motorbike and drove off for the station to check with the inspector if there had been any developments in the murder investigation. Pengelly said that, now that the time of death had been verified, it had been necessary to interview all of the cricketers, of both sides, to discover their whereabouts on the evening and night of the Friday prior to the match. He said that all had accepted the need for the additional questioning, all, of course, apart from Ian Friend. Surly as always the young miscreant felt that he was being singled out, and almost accused of the deed itself. Unfortunately he could not account for his whereabouts at the time in question, and his poor harassed parents were not prepared to give him an alibi. Robert thought that he had probably been out poaching somewhere.

Robert told the inspector of his conversation with Dave Chalmers, and asked him to find out the ownership of the mysterious forest adjoining his farm. When he told Pengelly of the teenagers' activities in the wood where the murder had taken place, the inspector smiled and said "Yes, our forensic boys have found evidence of these "Activities", and discounted them as having no bearing on the crime." He told Robert to carry on with his usual routine, just to keep a sharp eye to spot anything out of the ordinary going on." He said that murder squad detectives were coming down from London, and they would be talking to him and relying on him for his knowledge of the whole area.

For the rest of that afternoon the young policeman took time to go to each of his three villages, and to park his bike in order to stroll around and talk to the villagers. Being trusted and liked by the vast majority of them, he was able to assure them of their safety and confidently predict that the killer would soon be apprehended by his fellow officers. Nobody had reported anything strange of late, and there had been no strangers lurking around. Some of the Italian prisoners of war from the POW camp situated between Elwood and Hawksmead had been seen wandering about, and buying cigarettes in the local newsagents shop, but this was not unusual, in fact, these soldiers were quite popular with their peculiar way of talking. They all seemed to be happy, and indeed some had no desire to return to their home country, and talked of trying to remain in England. A few of the young ladies would probably welcome this Robert thought, and hoped that conflict would not develop between the prisoners and the local lads. So far all had been well. Having elicited no useful intelligence about the murder from his trip around his patch, he made his way back home, thinking that tomorrow he would visit all of the farmers on his patch, to see if they had any news for him.

Dave Chalmers owned the biggest farm by acreage in the district, but there were smaller units, some no bigger than large allotments. Many of the latter were no more than hobby farmers, having full or part-time jobs as well as tending to their small flocks of hens, geese or ducks, and rearing a few pigs. Robert set off in a methodical manner to see them all starting with those nearest to his house. At all of these enterprises he was received in a friendly manner, and the encounters were brief. After enquiring about their families and inevitably discussing the weather, talk was of the recent, violent event about which they had all heard. Only on one remote farm situated between the two villagers was anything untoward mentioned. This enterprise nestled high up the valley, and, because of the hilly terrain harboured a flock of Romney Marsh sheep, and some two hundred Sussex beef cattle with a huge, but thankfully gentle bull named Billy of course. The farmhouse itself was almost completely surrounded by an impressive array of oak, ash and beech trees, interspersed with hazel and holly. Grey squirrels, rabbits, little owls and badgers frequented this small wood.

Jim Bailey worked this farm with his wife Betty. They had twin boys, Alan and Terry aged seven now. A young couple, they both came from farming stock and worked hard to extract a reasonable living from their land. Invited in to the house, and given a welcome mug of tea, Robert asked how they were doing. They both expressed satisfaction at the way the farm was functioning, all animals fit and well, and the small acreage of barley looking well. The twin boys were already young farmers, and, on coming home from school, wasted no time in changing into work clothes and helping dad out. They had both extracted lambs from ewes that were struggling to give birth on their own and happily cared for young lambs whose mother had rejected them. The Baileys were a happy, hard-working family who deserved to succeed.

Robert asked if anything untoward had happened recently, and it was obvious that he was referring to the murder. Jim said that he was constantly pulling up rabbit snares in his little wood, and felt that Ian Friend was probably the culprit. These traps could cause an animal a long and agonising death, and Jim went on to say that he had once found a badger caught in one of them, and had had to kill it to release it from its agony. Robert nodded, for it was something he had to deal with frequently. He knew that Ian was not the only poacher in the area, and he had some sympathy with them, knowing that, with the rationing of food, a rabbit or two would be a welcome addition to a restricted diet. It was not unusual for him or Anne to find, on the doorstep a plump bunny, ready paunched, and waiting to be made in to a delicious pie.

As Robert was about to leave, Jim called to him "There was something else, which we found strange and a bit worrying. It was in that big forest up on the slope". He pointed over the stream and at the forest on the opposite side of the valley. Stepping off his bike Robert asked "What exactly happened Jim?" the young farmer thought for a minute then said "It was most peculiar and I'm not sure I can explain it to you. It was two Saturdays ago, late in the evening. I'd gone outside to check everything was ok, and to give the dogs a run before shutting up for the night. It was a beautiful evening, warm, with a little breeze from the west. The moon was up and there was barely a cloud in the sky. It was a typical summer night, peaceful and quiet, even the little owl had yet to wake up to search for a tasty meal. I just stood there taking in the view and the atmosphere and watching the bats flitting about searching for insects. I could see the lights in the village below in the valley, and the occasional headlights of a car moving along the valley road. Then I heard a strange noise coming from the direction of the forest. The dogs heard it too and pricked up their ears. It was not the sound of voices, but rather some sort of mechanical sound, a series of whistles and almost gurgles. I know it sounds daft, but it was a noise I'd never heard before. It wasn't particularly loud and only went on for a couple of minutes. I stood there for about maybe ten minutes, but the sounds were never repeated, and I've not heard them since even though I've made a point of going outside at the same time each evening since to hear any repetition of the unusual noise. I often walk round the bottom of the stand of trees with my dogs, but I've never seen or heard anything odd, only the once as I've explained". Robert knew that the farmer was a steady, sensible man, not given to flights of fancy, and he felt that he would have to report the conversation to the inspector.

That evening Robert went to the village pub, as was his wont, to meet up with his fellow cricketers for a chat and perhaps a game of darts. Talk was of course about the great game itself and of the test match currently being played. They all had their favourites, their heroes, and there was much good-natured banter when one of these individuals failed to score many runs, took no wickets, or, horror of horrors, dropped a catch. The sporting discussion over, Robert skilfully turned the conversation to the forest at the head of the valley. They all were aware of it because it dominated so much of the landscape. However no-one had anything of import to say about the wooded feature. The general opinion being that, since they were not allowed to enter it, they largely took little notice of it. Most regretted not being allowed to go for a stroll through the trees with the family on a Sunday afternoon. After a couple of pints of the landlord's best bitter, Robert bade farewell to his friends, saying that he would see them all at the next match, and left for home. When he mentioned Jim Bailey's report of strange sounds emanating from the trees, there was a shaking of heads, no-one had heard anything like this.

For the next few days Robert continued with his duties, calling at frequent intervals his station to see if they wanted him to do anything differently. He noticed the patrol cars circling round the area just as the inspector had promised. He had only one or two minor infractions of the law to deal with, mostly concerning youths with too much energy. With few people owning motor cars, most had a bicycle, even the older folk. Two or even three children on one bike was a fairly common sight, but a warning from Robert made them see sense, at least until the next time! He ignored Silly Bill's eccentric way of riding his bike. The old soldier had raised the saddle as far as possible so that, according to his sister Liz, he could see over hedges into peoples gardens. Bill often rode hands held aloft in the air, and, when Robert pointed to the handlebars, he would reply with an obscene gesture and a broad grin. The occasional army vehicle would sometimes roll through the village on its way to the prisoner's camp, taking provisions, and bringing men so that the guards could be rotated. Although the camp was outside of his jurisdiction, Robert made a point of going there weekly just to show his face. Seeing the Italian soldiers inside the prison reminded him of his time in their country when he wore the khaki uniform.

The inspector called for him to come to the station for an update on the investigation into the murder. On arrival he was introduced to two murder squad detectives from London. They questioned him at length about the district and the people who inhabited it. They felt that, since this was a quite remote area of the country, their first instinct was that the perpetrator might well be a local person. They asked him for the names of any characters who he thought could be capable of such a deed. They had noted the name of Ian Friend from the crime register. He was known to the police, had a record of transgressions, was belligerent, disliked the police, and, as a prolific poacher had a detailed knowledge of the countryside round about, and specifically the wood where the corpse had been found. Robert told the detectives that he didn't feel that Ian though admittedly a rogue, was capable of murder, but that, of course, was only his opinion.

The only other really odd character in the area was Silly Bill. The officers immediately showed an interest in him, and resolved to interview him as soon as possible. Silently Robert wished them the best of luck, but asked that they spoke to his sister first. Several cups of tea later, and the discussion over, Robert, Inspector Pengelly and the two detectives drove off to visit the scene of the murder. The two London men requested that they enter the wood alone while the local policemen remained in the car. The spot where the body had lain was clearly marked, and, through the trees Robert could see them methodically searching the undergrowth for any evidence. They explained that they were aware that Pengelly's men, and forensic teams, had already done finger-tip searches of the wood, but said that maybe new pairs of eyes might spot something which had been missed. The detectives spent upwards of an hour meticulously searching the wood and the field beyond it. At last they emerged, thanked the two officers for waiting so patiently, and suggested a visit to the pub was called for not only to quench thirsts, but to talk further about the investigation. As they entered the pub the locals eyed them with suspicion, but, when they went into the saloon bar for some privacy, the games of darts and dominoes carried on again. Over pints of beer, the local ale much appreciated by the London men, they discussed what steps next to take in their inquiry. Inspector Pengelly promised to produce a detailed map of the entire area, and Robert offered to take the two around the district in one of the patrol cars, showing them where certain people lived. Feeling that they had done all they could for the present, the inspector drove them all back to the station, where Robert retrieved his motorbike and returned home.

CHAPTER SEVEN

If he was thinking of a peaceful evening with Anne and little Emily, Robert was mistaken. A frantic banging on the door disturbed their quiet time together. On opening the door he discovered a distraught and tearful Liz, Bill's sister, talking in a high-pitched voice at such a speed that no sense could be made of her burbling. Fortunately Anne had come to the door. She took Liz's hand and led her into the kitchen, sat her down and gently calmed her down, so that eventually they could understand what had so agitated her. A cup of sweet tea completed the soothing down, and Liz could now explain what had upset her so. She said that two policemen, obviously the two detectives, had come to her cottage, and had tried to ask her brother questions in a very aggressive manner. Bill, she said, had simply looked bewildered, and had brushed past the men, mouthing unintelligibly, had grabbed his beloved bike and disappeared at great speed. She was worried as to where he might have gone, and he had not taken the tablets which kept him reasonably calm. Robert promised to find her brother, and, leaving her with Anne, he set off on his motor bike looking for the slightly unhinged veteran. He too was angry and vowed to have words with the insensitive officers who had handled the situation so clumsily.

He knew that Bill would seek the sanctuary of trees, and set off to look in the, unfortunately, numerous woods in the district. Riding through the village he saw Brian Morgan, out walking with his wife and springer spaniel. Indignantly Brian said that Bill had gone racing past them, narrowly missing his dog. He pointed in the direction the cyclist had gone, and said that the policeman should have a word with him about his behaviour on the lanes. Thanking him Robert continued with his search going in the direction indicated by his fellow cricketer. He was now going towards Jim Bailey's farm, and felt that the little stand of trees on his farm might well be where Bill was hiding. Jim's wife, Betty, told Robert that her husband had gone to the pub for a drink with his mates. She said that she had not seen Bill, but that she had been in the house all evening. Thanking her he set off through the farm yard, and across the meadow to the trees. As he entered the wood he called out saying who he was, and looking for sign that the old man was hiding there. Hearing a sobbing noise he walked towards it, and sitting with his back to a beech tree was Bill, his bike leaning against the other side of the tree. Tears were streaming down his cheeks, and he looked terrified.

Without talking Robert sat beside him and took his hand. "Bill," he said quietly, "I'm sorry about those two men frightening you. They've gone now, and I will make certain that they will not annoy you again. You are not in any sort of trouble I promise you." A rare smile came across Bill's face, and he squeezed Robert's hand. "Shall we go back home now Bill, your sister is worried about you." After some hesitation, the old poacher slowly got up, grabbed his bicycle and, mounting it, set off through the trees, across the meadow and through the farmyard to the lane. Running after him, Robert reached the lane to see Bill racing away pedalling like mad. He knew that the old man would go home, so he went to his house to tell Liz that he had found her brother, and that he was not harmed in any way. He walked with Liz to her cottage to ascertain that her brother had got home safely, and, seeing his trusty bike leant against the wall, they knew that he was indeed back home. The policeman left the two damaged souls in peace, knowing that there was little more he could do that evening. When he got home Anne could see how angry he was at the treatment of the mentally damaged old soldier. She hugged him and said that, in the morning she would go to see that Liz and Bill were ok.

Robert was up early the next morning. After a hurried breakfast, he took Meg for her usual run, then returned home to don his uniform and say farewell to Anne and Emily. At the station he bade a gruff good morning to the desk sergeant who looked surprised as Robert was an old friend and always an affable fellow. However today the village bobby was in a mood of cold fury. He marched into the room which had been set aside for the murder team. The two detectives were sitting at a large table examining an assortment of papers strewn haphazardly across it. Both were smoking cigarettes and the room was becoming increasingly foggy. There were no windows open, and Robert quickly remedied that opening them as wide as possible. The London men looked warily at Robert realising that all was not well. DC Malcolm Alvey pushed his chair back, stubbed out his cigarette and spoke. "What's got you out of bed the wrong side today Mister Evans?" Ignoring the chair which DC Trevor Bailey offered him, Robert, speaking with barely suppressed anger said "I won't have arrogant officers like you bullying and frightening my people." "Oh", said Alvey "you mean the idiot Bill and his pathetic sister." Trying to choose his words carefully Robert said quietly "Bill is not an idiot, and Liz is one of the most respected ladies in the village. I told you to handle them with great care, but instead you blundered in and frightened the life out of them, and, as a result, I had to spend a great deal of time looking for the confused old man, while my wife had to comfort Liz."

The two detectives looked at one another, and it was Bailey, clearing his throat said "From what you had told us this Silly Bill was one of the two people liable to act strangely. We thought it essential to go in hard to see if we could learn something from him. In hindsight we now realise we handled it the wrong way, we'll go and see them and apologise". "No you won't" said Robert "If you go anywhere near them Bill will certainly run away. Apart from telling the time always the same time, he has not spoken for years now, and he probably never will. And there's no good asking him to write anything down as he is illiterate." Inspector Pengelly had been listening to the raised voices, and he now entered the room. Addressing the detectives he said "From now on only Robert will have any dealings with Liz and her brother. I think you can see that nothing will be gained by interviewing them again". The two Londoners looked at one another and Trevor Bailey replied "Ok we are sorry we were little hasty in going so quickly to see Bill, but we wanted to see if we could ruffle a few feathers early in our investigation, and we still feel that our murderer is probably a local. The scene of the crime is pretty remote, and the only people who know of its location are farmers, farm workers and the people of the two villages. I promise you that from now on we will rely on you Robert to advise us before we take any further action." Mollified Robert thanked them and, together with the inspector sat down to look at all of the papers assembled on the desk. With the air cleared the officers could now put forward their ideas on how to proceed with the investigation.

DC Alvey said that they had circulated a picture of the victim to the police forces of other nations, and had especially pointed out the scarring on her back, with the possible "c" showing. Thus far they had not received any feedback but it was early days yet. He said that they would like to talk to Ian Friend, and asked the local policemen to tell them about him, and where they were likely to find him this morning. Robert told them that he was a general farm worker, and went from farm to farm wherever there was work for him. He explained that, although he was a bit of a rogue, he was actually a good worker and could turn his hand to practically anything on the farm. "He's a strong lad", said Robert, "and a good all-round sportsman, excelling at cricket and football. He's also an accomplished darts player until he's had a few. He doesn't like authority, particularly policemen, and will have a belligerent attitude, but he's not really violent. Nobody knows the woods like him, and, if you can get him on your side, he could prove useful in helping you to better understand the area."

With a much more congenial atmosphere now established, helped out by mugs of tea, the discussion ended. Inspector Pengelly ordered that there should be daily meetings to pool ideas and to discuss the case whether there had been any appreciable progress or not. Robert set off on his daily rounds, and was gratified when old Bill actually gave him a friendly wave as he passed him. He would not be in the least surprised if a plump rabbit did not materialise on his doorstep in the very near future.

As he returned home for lunch, he was surprised to see a patrol car parked outside his house. Om entering he saw seated in the kitchen the two detectives, drinking tea and eating one of Anne's delicious rock cakes. Trevor was reading one of Emily's story books to her, while Meg sat at the officer's feet, ears cocked, listening as the tale was unfolded. It was Malcolm who explained why they were here. "We're sorry to intrude on your home, and to disturb your beautiful wife, but we felt that we needed to talk to you urgently." Realising that it would be police matters, Anne took Emily out of the kitchen, with Trevor promising to read the rest of the story to her some other time. "We've been to see your friend Ian, and got absolutely nowhere. As you said he doesn't like the police, and refused to say anything. But when we told him that we could take him to the station to interview him, he said that he would only talk to his local bobby, that Evans fellow". "He'll be in the Kings Arms this evening as usual, and I'll talk to him there" said Robert." If I go to his house, his parents and older brother will be there, and they are all as anti the police as he is. It might cost me a pint or two to soften his attitude towards me, but it might be worth it." Satisfied the duo left, thanking Anne for her hospitality, and returned to the station. Robert could now relax and have a quiet lunch with his family.

After a routine afternoon where he stopped frequently to chat to local people, all well known to him, Robert went home to play in the garden with Emily and Meg, while Anne prepared dinner. He often marvelled how his wife could serve up delicious meals day by day despite the rationing which obtained, and which apparently would continue for years yet. As he tucked into an appetising rabbit pie, he could not help but feel a little guilty since the meat had been donated by a criminal, although he baulked at calling Bill a criminal. He often wondered how many other people had enjoyed the fruits of such criminality, and silently he thanked Silly Bill for his generosity. Ian Friend had never left rabbits on his doorstep, but maybe there were other members of the community whose diets had been helped by him too. Having helped Anne with the washing up, and after reading a bedtime story to Emily, Robert set off to walk to the Kings Arms, on his way pondering how best to talk to the aggressive fast bowler.

As ever the pub was full, and he exchanged banter with everybody. The cricketers were looking forward to their next match, against a team from the nearby town, whose umpire was known to favour his own side very much. Unfortunately most of the players of the town side were relatives of the said umpire. A win against this lot would indeed be a near miracle. However the dreaded official always carried a hip flask of whisky, and, if you were fortunate enough to be stationed at square leg, you would be offered a generous swig. Many a young fielder had had to be guided back to the pavilion after a hot afternoon in convivial conversation with the crafty umpire. Losing a game through drunkenness was not a result recognised by Wisden.

Ian Friend was leaning on the bar near the dartboard cigarette in hand. Approaching him Robert asked him if they could have a chat. "Ah, if you buy me a pint" said the surly young man. Drinks in hand the two went into the empty saloon bar and sat down in comfortable armchairs. Ian fidgeted for a while in his seat waiting for the policeman to open the conversation. Clearing his throat Robert said "You know that I am not here to accuse you of anything, but rather we are seeking your help to find out who killed the young woman in the wood. I understand why you did not want to speak to the two detectives from London, and they are more than happy to leave it to me to talk to you about your night-time activities". At that Friend bridled and got up to leave the room, but, hastily Robert spoke further "Hang on Ian, this is not about your poaching, it's rather about your knowledge of the countryside round about, and particularly the wooded areas. We don't want to know how many rabbits and other animals and birds you've caught recently, but we need to know if you have seen anything untoward, any strangers or strange noises. Have you seen any vehicles, apart from the usual ones, travelling the lanes in the hours of darkness?" He went on to say that they had not, as yet, found out the identity of the victim, and he did not mention the weird scarring on the girl's back. Mollified Ian took another draught of his ale and said "I only usually run across old Bill, and he only glares at me, I suppose because I'm taking prey which he thinks belongs to him. You never do him for poaching do you?" Robert smiled and replied "Would there be any point Ian?" The burly young miscreant almost smiled, and nodded in agreement. They sat supping their beer for a while when Ian said "There's one odd thing, sometimes when I'm in the big stand of trees behind the church, I can see flickering lights which seem to be coming from the POW's camp. I always thought that lights in the billets had to be put out at ten o'clock. The lights I saw were not those of the perimeter security lamps, and these unusual lights don't last for long. Since they don't interfere with me, I just ignore them". Robert thanked him for the information, and, while going to the bar to refill their glasses, he thought that he must pay the camp a visit shortly. He did occasionally stop off there on his rounds to chat to the guards, but the camp was the responsibility of the army, and he had no jurisdiction inside the tall fences.

He returned to the saloon where Ian was still seated, looking more relaxed now that he knew that he was not, for the moment, in trouble. They now talked cricket and discussed their forthcoming games at the weekend. Ian smiled when he learned of Robert's opponents and their umpire. Then looking down almost apologetically, he said "Sorry about that bouncer I bowled at you last weekend, but you didn't have to hit the next ball quite so hard!" They both grinned and Robert said "If I hadn't hit it so far we wouldn't have found the girl. "He got up to leave asking Ian to let him know if he had any more information to give him, and he warned "You be careful now, remember there's a murderer somewhere out there."

CHAPTER EIGHT

With the weekend approaching all was now quiet. Robert continued with his patrols finding that the parishioners were ever more eager to talk to him, perhaps seeking further reassurance. They were eager to tell him who, or what sort of person would commit murder, and, inevitably fingers were pointed at Silly Bill, who, until now they had all thought of him as harmless. Some people thought he should look closely at the Italian POWs since they seemed to go and please as they wished. Even the vicar had his own ideas about the crime. As ever rumours abounded throughout the area. Reporters from the local and national papers invaded the district, and cameramen took numerous photos of woods, trees, animals and of the villagers. Sales of the local and national newspapers went sky-high, and the excitement which Robert had hoped would soon abate, was rekindled. Most people welcomed the frenzied activity, it added colour to their normal humdrum lives.

However two people were not happy with the newspapermen. Robert knew that at some time the reporters would want to interview Bill, and he stationed himself outside Liz's cottage as often as he could to prevent the two vulnerable people being tormented by unscrupulous hacks. One belligerent crime reporter tried to insist on being allowed to talk to the old couple. Robert explained that Bill could not talk, and that his sister had already been traumatised by the visit of the two detectives. Sensing a good, human interest scoop, the reporter tried to force his way into the house. The policeman quickly restrained him, gently put him on the ground and told him to leave or be arrested for trespass. Picking himself up the irate man went back to his car threatening to report Robert for assault. Fortunately Inspector Pengelly backed up his colleague, and warned the man to be careful how he approached the villagers. To emphasise his dislike of the man's bullish attitude, Pengelly then proceeded to closely examine the newsman's car, noting the lack of tread on two of the tyres, and one defective side light. Suitably chastened and promising to see to the work which needed doing to his automobile, the reporter hastily left the district, snarling at the two coppers he could see grinning in his rear view mirror.

One duty which Robert never failed to fulfil was his weekly visit to the Brisley sisters, Maud and Charlotte. This venerable old couple, now well into their eighties, lived on a smallholding of perhaps three or so acres between the two villagers, on a small hillock which gave them spectacular views over the whole valley. They had inherited the little farm from their parents, long since now gone. To describe them as old-fashioned would be an understatement. When a supply of electricity was finally brought to the settlements, they had stubbornly refused to have anything to do with it, believing it to be unnatural and against God's law. Like their mother and father they were regular churchgoers, and, apart from visits to the village shops, rarely ventured out of their cottage. Elderly they might be but they were fully compos mentis, and, from their lofty vantage point, could see most of what went on in the valley, and on the slopes leading up to the various woods, and the POW camp. Like all who lived on the land their lives were dominated by their animals, a few heifers, their ducks, geese and their two dogs. Robert would help each summer with the hay-making, often assisted by the farmer Dave Chalmers. He would bring a tractor and a wain to fork up the hay. Then, under the watchful eyes of the sisters they would pile it up in the barn. Jugs of sweet well water were given to the harvesters to refresh them, as again the Brisleys would not have mains water brought to their land. Payment for the men's labour was always bottles of Guinness. One winter, in the early morning hours of a particularly snowy January night, Maud, the older sister, fetched Robert to help one of her heifers which was in trouble having a calf. Arriving at the cowshed, Maud hung up a lantern to light the scene, and then scurried off into the house, leaving him to it. After some twenty minutes of pulling and straining, he, and the cow managed to produce a healthy bull calf. While fully occupied in the strenuous procedure in the shed, Robert was aware of the two dogs in the house barking incessantly. The successful birthing done, he went to the house to tell them of the new birth. Accepting the mandatory bottle of Guinness, he asked what had disturbed the dogs. Charlotte replied "We make them bark so we can't hear the poor cow hollering". Robert walked back home chuckling to himself, and saying "I must tell them one day that I hate bloody Guinness!"

He opened the old wrought iron gate to the Brisley's cottage with its squeaky hinge and walked along the brick pathway, bordered on the one side by a multitude of rose bushes with a profusion of blooms, emanating a sweet, almost overpowering scent as he passed. On the other side of the path was a large pond on which lazily swam beautifully coloured ducks and drakes, while, on the edges of the water a pair of geese were haughtily preening themselves, looking disdainfully at their smaller cousins in the pond, wasting energy on this glorious day. A towering willow bent graciously towards the water, creating a cool shady area. The surface of the pond shimmered in the glaring rays of the sun. Robert paused for long moments taking in the beauty and tranquillity of the scene. The sisters were certainly fortunate to live in such glorious surroundings.

He knocked on the old iron studded door and waited for the sound of numerous locks and chains being undone. Then, before opening, a querulous voice asked "Who is it?", "It's only the policeman" said Robert, a smile on his face. "Are you sure?" came back the response. "Yes Maud, it is me as usual." The door could now be opened wide, and Maud, with Charlotte close behind her, welcomed him in. He loved this old cottage, it was like returning to what he imagined life was like in the time of Queen Victoria. He went into a wood panelled hallway with a picture of an ancient bearded postman, wearing a smart cap and carrying his mail sack on his shoulder with the caption "Mail at last".

Removing his helmet he followed the sisters into perhaps his favourite room of all time. Dark, but not gloomy, the only light coming from the small window with its chintz curtains, ceiling so low that Robert had to stoop slightly to avoid hitting his head on the old wooden beams. A stone floor with obviously home-made rugs scattered about, and on these were curled up an assortment of multi-coloured cats, oblivious to the visit of the law man. On the whitewashed walls black and white prints depicting scenes which seemed to come from the novels of Charles Dickens. In front of the fire a shiny brass fender, and a trivet on which stood a large kettle. The room was almost suffocatingly warm as the fire was always lit regardless of the temperature outside. Maud left the room through a heavy oak door, and returned carrying a tray on which were cups and saucers with a flowery pattern, and a teacup, milk jug and tea pot, matching the decoration on the cups and saucers. She poured out the drinks, offered Robert a slice of cake, and the three sat in the comfortably over-stuffed armchairs. Looking at the two sisters, he thought, in all the time he had known them, they had never changed. Older certainly, and a little more lined of face, they could only have been sisters. Both only a pinch above five feet in height, and slim of build, they remained robustly active despite their advancing years. Charlotte's brown locks were only recently showing streaks of white, and she was always well-groomed. Maud was never seen without the battered old black hat she wore now, even in her own sitting room. Some cynics in the village said that she was probably bald, and that she never went out when there was a strong wind! Eccentric the two ladies might be, but they were well liked in the village, and were a common sight cycling to the local shops on their old trade's bikes to fetch food and other provisions, usually with their dogs running alongside them.

Reclining in his armchair, with one of the cats purring softly as it took advantage of the warmth of his lap, Robert rather hesitantly asked the ladies if they had seen or heard anything unusual lately. The problem with asking this question was that, to the venerable duo, anything slightly modern was, to them, not only unusual, but positively unworldly. Their first sighting of a tractor had them hurrying to Robert to report a strange and noisy machine frightening their animals. During the war years they had dug their own shelter in the back garden, and had ventured from it only to see to their cattle and birds. The doodlebug which had been shot down early one morning in the summer of 1944 had nearly given the sisters heart attacks. They owned an old hammer shotgun, licensed of course, and Maud could not resist taking a pot-shot at any aeroplane which dared to fly over their own part of the sky, friendly or enemy crafts, it made no difference to her, and fortunately she had no chance of bringing one of them down. All the while she was hurling abuse at the pilot in a language totally unsuited to a lady.

It was Maud who answered, while Charlotte occasionally chipped in with her own thoughts. "We don't like those Italian prisoners roaming about in the village. They should stay locked up. One of them came here looking for work, and we had to threaten him with the dogs", "I even fetched the shotgun" put in Charlotte. "Don't know why they aren't sent back where they came from", continued Maud. Encouraging her to talk on, Robert said "Anything else worrying you both?" It was now Charlotte who spoke. Going to the little window, she pointed up the hill towards the great stand of trees which dominated the landscape. "Some nights" she almost whispered, "we hear strange noises coming from there, and flickering lights, like people waving torches about. We thought at first that it might he old Bill poaching his rabbits, but once, when the twittering noises were being made, we saw Bill standing by his bike in the lane listening like us to the weird sounds". On his evening patrols Robert could see how, on dark, moonless nights the towering trees of Oak Hill took on an aura of menace, and could see why people gave them a wide berth. He thanked the women for their hospitality, and rose from his seat, much to the annoyance of his adopted cat. Regretfully he had to decline the offer of a bottle of Guinness, saying that he was not allowed to drink while on duty.

CHAPTER NINE

After breakfast on Saturday morning, he called the station to see if there had been any further developments before signing off for a relaxing weekend with his family, and looking forward to the game of cricket that afternoon. He walked down to the newsagents with Emily and Meg, greeting people as he went. The women fussed over his daughter saying how pretty she was, and how like her mum she was. A mandatory stop at the bridge over the stream to see the little fishes and the ducks swimming sedately with the gentle current, then to the shop to buy his local paper. He normally turned first to the sports pages to see how the local town cricket team was doing, but today his eye was caught by the headlines on the front page. There was a picture of the face of the girl found in the wood with a caption "Does anyone know this young lady?" Then followed an article all about the murder, some accurate but, as usual, some simply speculating as to the identity of the victim and her assailant and the possible reason for such a horrendous attack. Further down the page was a photo of Robert and Inspector Pengelly, "The officers who, we confidently predict, will soon have the vicious brute behind bars". There was no mention of the scarring on the girl's back. When Emily saw the picture of her dad she squealed with excitement, and could not wait to get home to show her mum. Anne too was impressed by the photo of her husband and flirtingly remarked "And to think I'm married to such a handsome hero!"

Before lunch Robert decided to ring the station once again in light of the newspaper article. He wanted to know if there had been any reaction from the readers of the paper. The desk sergeant could only tell him that, apart from the usual cranks, nothing of interest had been reported. From the numerous phone calls received at the station, it appeared that the general consensus was that it was aliens who had carried out the dastardly deed or members of some obscure religious cult. The sergeant told him that the two detectives had gone home for the weekend, and that the murder had been reported in most of the national papers. These, with a wider circulation, had also mentioned the scarring, asking if anyone might recognise it. For the cranks this was fertile ground, and theories about the scars were numerous and outlandish, and usually concerned creatures from an alien planet.

Feeling that no more could be done today, Robert now set about having a relaxing day, spending quality time with his two favourite ladies, enjoying a pleasant lunch outside on the lawn, and then strolling down to the cricket field for an afternoon's game of his favourite sport. Today no Ian Friend, trying to knock his head off, rather a dodgy umpire, and a team eager to defeat them in the glorious conflict to come.

It was an afternoon made for cricket. A wonderful setting, the summer green of the trees and grass lit spectacularly by the welcoming sun. As he walked down towards the ground, Robert felt that this could only be England, an England now freed from the shackles of a devastating war, and hopefully looking to a bright future. As he thought about the battles in which he had fought as a soldier, a frown came across his normally cheerful features, but he shook his head, preparing himself for a very different battle to come, where bullets, bombs and shells were replaced by an innocuous little red ball. He was the first of the participants to arrive, but the pavilion was open and he could leave his gear in his usual place in the home dressing room (always the same place as, like many sportsmen he was superstitious). He now walked along the boundary to greet Pip, Squeak and Wilfred, the faithful old soldiers who rarely missed a match .The trio were already ensconced in their deckchairs, Pip quickly into snooze mode. The two awake veterans wished him good luck while Pip grunted something unintelligible. Robert wondered what the old codgers did in the winter months with no cricket to watch.

He now walked out to the wicket where he placed the stumps in their rightful positions and carefully walked down the hallowed wicket trying to gauge how it might play today. There had been little rain lately and there would be plenty of bounce from the fast bowlers. Thoughtfully he stood there wondering how many people had played the great game here, sadly some of the men from the village had died in the two world wars, and their names were recorded in the pavilion. Some of the ancients of the village said that the great W G Grace himself had shown off his unmatchable skills on this very pitch.

Players from both sides now began to drift in, greeting each other amicably. Apart from some of the youngsters, they all knew each other having battled over the years on this ground, and on the opposition's field in the town. Robert's picture in the paper caused ribald comment with "Can I have your autograph constable?" It was all done in a good-natured way and he only smiled as he retorted "It'll cost you!" In the changing room there was the same banter initially, and he was asked if there had been any progress in the investigation. Given a negative response, minds were now concentrated on the serious business of the forthcoming contest. Brian said "We're mostly up against the same old bunch, except two young lads I've never played against before." Laughingly Robert asked "They're not, I hope relatives of the umpire!" The smiles which accompanied that remark had a touch of worry or apprehension in them.

Having won the toss, the home side decided to bat first. Although it was still a bright and sunny day, there was a build-up of ominously looking clouds looming over the hills. Padded up, Robert and Brian strode out to the wicket accompanied by clapping from the few spectators who had come to watch the game. Brian took first strike, and his opening partner stood at the non-striker's end with the biased umpire. The latter greeted Robert and took from his pocket a pair of spectacles with very thick lenses. Squinting short-sightedly at Robert he said "That's better, I didn't realise how poor my eyesight had become lately". Robert strolled slowly down the wicket, prodding it gently as he walked, and whispered to Brian "Whatever you do don't get your pads in the way, or you're buggered." Brian kept the strike for a few overs accumulating fifteen runs, until it was Robert's turn to face the bowling. Before starting his long run-up, the fast bowler shouted "Mind that wood behind me Bob!" which brought gales of laughter from the fielders and the two umpires.

Fifty up, the two openers were now feeling comfortable and a big total beckoned. Then tragedy struck. Brian nicked an away swinger from the left arm bowler, and the ball went straight to second slip who promptly dropped it. The bowler made a loud half appeal, cutting it off as he saw the chance missed. He then saw that the bespectacled umpire had his finger raised signifying out. "It's OK ump, he's dropped it" said the bowler. The dreaded finger remained raised and the short-sighted official stated with pompous authority "I've given the batsman out LBW." Brian looked incredulously down the pitch, then without demur he strode off to the pavilion, thunderous of face, but never thinking of questioning the decision of the official. There was embarrassment on the faces of the fielding side especially the butter-fingered slip fielder but the game must continue, and fortunately the incident did not spoil the friendly but competitive nature of the contest.

The innings continued with runs being steadily compiled but wickets falling at regular intervals. Fortunately there were no more iffy decisions, all the wickets clean bowled or caught. However Robert continued to bat on, reaching his fifty to the applause of his teammates, and the three deckchair dwellers, all of whom had now donned pullovers as the sun was beginning to disappear behind the rolling clouds. It looked as though a period of rain was now imminent. With solid runs behind him, and the threat of weather perhaps stopping play, Robert decided to open his shoulders in the quest to get runs quickly. A pull over mid-wicket, a leg glance, and several classy cover drives saw him near a century. With the scoreboard now showing ninety six runs against his name, he was served up a juicy half volley by the quick bowler. One pace down the wicket, a flowing swing of the bat, and the ball soared over the bowler's head straight towards the ill-fated wood. Luckily, this time it landed just short of the boundary, but proceeded to bounce over the lane and into the trees. The fielder at long on yelled at Robert "I'm not going in there Bob, you can fetch it, you hit it!" There was general merriment, and all watched as an intrepid lad raced into the wood to emerge with the ball held triumphantly in his hand. Now there was applause for the century, and the skipper declared the innings closed. As he walked off Emily, together with Meg, ran to greet her daddy and to give him sloppy kisses as Anne proudly clapped her husband back to the pavilion.

Unfortunately the rain which had threatened all afternoon eventually arrived a short time after the opposition had started their innings. They had lost quick wickets, and a victory seemed almost certain. After sitting disappointedly in their respective changing rooms waiting for the rain to cease, both sides decided to abandon the match. It being too early for the pub to open, the players all went home wishing each other well, and hoping to have better luck with the weather next year. As the rain grew steadily harder, Robert walked the short distance to his home with Anne, Emily, and a bedraggled Meg. It had been an unsatisfactory day's cricket for the teams, but for Robert his century was the highlight of his season thus far. Only poor Brian "Umpired out" had real cause to feel aggrieved. The trio of elderly supporters had adjourned to the pavilion to escape the rain, but had then reluctantly left the ground to make their way home, each with sandwiches and cakes given to them by the lovely ladies in charge of refreshments.

Sunday dawned bright and sunny once more. Yesterday's rain had freshened the air and the sultriness of the last few days had dissipated. One quick call to the station was all the work that Robert would do today. His parents were coming for lunch, and as usual he peeled the potatoes, and prepared the rest of the vegetables, but left the cooking to his wife whose culinary skills were well known. He was playing in the garden with Emily when Gary and Jean Evans rolled up in their old Singer motor car. It had been a short journey from the other end of the village, and easily walkable, but Robert's mother suffered from arthritis, and walking pained her. Greetings over, and much fussing over their granddaughter, they all sat in the garden where Anne brought them tea and biscuits. Meg sat in front of them, and was rewarded with her customary treat before going to lie down in the shade. Initially the talk was of the weather, the latest news, rationing and the health of relatives and friends. Then Gary broached the subject of his son's work, and inevitably of the recent murder. He said that, having lived all of his life in the area, he had never heard of such an incident before. Even through the long war years nobody had been killed, or seriously hurt.

Feeling that the two men wanted to talk of more weighty matters, the ladies, together with Emily and Meg announced that they were going to take a walk down to the stream to see the ducks and fishes. Robert told his father of the progress, or rather lack of it, in the murder investigation. He asked his dad to tell him everything he knew about the area, and specifically about the war years, and the time since the cessation of hostilities. Firstly he wanted to know more about the POW camp. Dad said that there was an old army encampment on that spot, used to house soldiers waiting to go to France to fight in the trenches. It had been resurrected early in the 1940s, then encompassed by the existing wire fence, with guard posts at regular intervals. The first prisoners had arrived in the winter of 1943, he thought, and initially they had been confined to the barracks, and threatened with severe punishment should they try to escape. It was only as the war drew to an end that some of the POWs were allowed to leave the camp under a strict curfew. Some had helped out on the local farms, and farmers like Dave Chalmers had welcomed their assistance at busy times like hay-making and harvesting. In the village itself there was some hostility when the young men objected to the local girls showing interest in the prisoners. However they were generally well behaved and the villagers became used to seeing them walking about. Robert could confirm that saying to his father that he had not had any problems with the foreign soldiers. Next he asked his dad about characters in the two villagers, seeking his opinion as to whether any of the natives could, by any stretch of the imagination, be capable of a vicious attack on a young woman .Gary laughed "Most of the men round here wouldn't have the energy to do something energetic like that. Lifting a pint of beer in the Kings Arms is about all they can manage". He went on to add that in this close-knit community, everyone knew everyone else, and strangers were easily spotted, and often treated with suspicion. As the village bobby Robert could confirm that there had not been a burglary in the area for some time, and that poaching was the principle infringement hereabouts.

CHAPTER TEN

"What about the huge wood that's now fenced off with notices saying PRIVATE PROPERTY TRESPASSERS WILL BE PROSECUTED, Robert asked his father. "Now that is rather strange "replied the latter "when it was owned by Dave Chalmers, we used to play there regularly, and he didn't mind. We used to look for birds' nests there, build tree houses, and play hide and seek, and cowboys and Indians. Truth to tell I kissed a girl there for the first time, and it wasn't your mum. I know that there were pheasants, woodcocks, and of course pigeons in the wood, and Dave would invite fellow farmers to join him in rough shoots during the shooting season. It's a lovely wood with some very old oak, ash and beech trees, and everyone was surprised when Dave sold it. I believe it was bought by a foreign syndicate, but they don't seem to do anything with it, and now, with those fences round it and rather threatening posters, it seems a bit forbidding." Robert asked if he thought Silly Bill had tried to enter the wood since the erection of the fences, knowing that he would not be able to read the warning notices. "Very probably "replied Gary, "but I don't really know cos' he doesn't speak. I do know that, before the present set-up he used to catch rabbits, and pigeons in there. Now, when he cycles past it, he gives it two fingers, and shouts something unintelligible at it. You know, old Bill was something of a hero in the Great War. He was in it right from the start. For two and a half years he suffered the privations of life in the trenches, and was made a sergeant as a reward for his courage under fire. He was an example to his men, always encouraging them, and worrying about their welfare. But even for a stoical man like Bill, the constant danger, the appalling conditions in the trenches, and seeing his men horribly wounded and sometimes killed took their toll on his mental reserves. The final straw for him was being buried for hours when an artillery shell collapsed the sides of his trench. Though physically unhurt the dreadful experience unhinged him, and he was invalided out of the army. As a soldier, and a young man Bill was a strapping six-footer, good at sports and of a sunny disposition. But look at him now, unkempt and gaunt, and unable to speak for nearly thirty years now. Fortunately he has his sister Liz to care for him now".

Robert asked his father why he could only say that particular time, but Gary was unable to give a definitive answer saying only that it was obviously a specific time when something extraordinary had happened to him, but since he didn't speak they would probably never know the answer .Gary paused thinking about the past, and as they both looked towards the trees the word "forbidding" seemed an apposite description of the wood, and Robert resolved to see if he could discover more about it.

The walkers having returned from the stream, the family settled down to a pleasant afternoon chatting, and enjoying the warm summer sun. Under the proud eyes of the adults, Emily had a pretend tea party with a bemused Meg as her guest. As the sun began to drop below the horizon, and the warmth of the day began to fade, Gary and Jean left in their trusty old car to go to the evensong service at St Michaels, before going home. For Robert the visit of his mum and dad had been the perfect end to a relaxing weekend, despite the disappointment of the unfinished cricket match. As he drifted off to sleep on that barmy Sunday evening he wondered with some trepidation what the next day, and indeed the next week would bring.

Monday morning again dawned bright and fair, and as he stepped outside to greet the new day Robert breathed in the warm scents of summer, and listened to the songbirds chirruping, and the bees buzzing round the garden flowers. He compared all of this beauty to the ugliness of the scene in the wood recently. With a resolve to face the day positively, whatever it might bring, he mounted his motorbike and sped off to the station in the town.

Inspector Pengelly was waiting for him in the interview room set aside for the inquiry into the murder. He told Robert that there had been no new developments, but they would need to await the arrival of the detectives before they knew any more. The inspector reported that they continued to receive letters and phone calls from people insisting that they had important information to give, but, as ever, nothing useful was garnered. The business of the scarring had still not been made public, since that would cause even more speculation. Robert pointed out that the national newspapers had mentioned this so many of the villagers would be aware of it.

The London duo duly arrived and the now foursome could compare notes. Unfortunately the detectives could advance the investigation not much further. Police forces all over the country and law enforcement agencies abroad had all been asked if they could help. The concentration had been on the scarring, but no-one had been able to come up with an explanation, although there were many theories as to its meaning, and why it had been done. Robert was asked to simply continue with his usual duties, but keeping his ear to the ground for anything out of the ordinary. The detectives were still of the opinion that there was a local connection somewhere, but Robert remained sceptical. They said that they would continue to talk to local people but promised to put their questions sympathetically, so that he would not have a torrent of complaints from his fellow country-dwellers. He said that today, as he passed the POW camp, he might call in to chat with the guards to see how the inmates of the prison were behaving. Pengelly strongly warned him not to enter the camp, but to leave any investigation within the fence to his superiors and to the military authorities. Robert rather resented that order as he was quite aware of the bounds of his authority. The two detectives had themselves noted his irritation, and Trevor remarked that the inspector seemed to be a little riled at his and Malcolm's present here, perhaps feeling that he was more than capable of dealing with the death of the young lady.

So it was after lunch, his patrol having been duly completed, that he parked his motor outside the formidable gates of the detainment centre, and rang the bell to summon one of the sentries. Having been in the army himself, he had a certain affinity with the custodians, and knew most of them by name. It was Corporal Dicky Smith who answered his call, and, seeing Robert, he smiled broadly and opened the little side gate to let the officer in. He was particularly pleased to see Dicky, as he was one of the longest serving men at the camp. A cockney, and one of the shortest soldiers Robert had ever seen. He was ever cheerful and friendly, but his happy-go-lucky demeanour hid a sharp and penetrative mind, and he would know everything which went on within the boundaries of the camp. The two men went into the guardroom, exchanging pleasantries as they walked. Firstly Robert must sign the visitors book, policeman or not. Mugs of strong tea reminded Robert of the old NAAFIs in which he had spent many an enjoyable hour with fellow sprogs like Dicky. For a while they reminisced over the war days as old soldiers are wont to do. They had both been infantrymen, squaddies or PBIs, but Dicky, unlike Robert had come through the conflict unharmed. He had not been involved in the Italian campaign, but had fought through France and in to Germany. He had witnessed the horrors of Belsen, and said that the images of that dreadful place would stay with him for ever. Dicky said that he, and the other guards got on well with the Italian prisoners, or, at least most of them. He had the impression that most of them, if not all, hadn't wanted to fight in the war, and had gladly surrendered at the first opportunity. Although they all wanted to go home as soon as possible, they were satisfied with their treatment here in England, and were more than happy to help the farmers out when the need arose. Since the commanding officer of the establishment was rarely present, a Warrant Officer was effectively in charge, but he spent much of his time in the guard post doing crosswords, and picking winners at the horse racing.

Dicky said "I said most of the inmates were easy-going but there is one bunch who don't fit in with the others. There's just one hut with about twenty men in it, right up at the end of the compound where the inhabitants are a surly bunch, mostly staying in their billet all day, and only coming out for meals, and an occasional exercise walk round the facility. The other men say they all come from the north of Italy, and speak what sounds like a form of German. They ignore the other prisoners and stick closely together. They never take their shirts off to sunbathe, but rather are always in uniform, and appear to obey the orders of a huge man sporting the three stripes of a sergeant. They never leave the camp, and, when one of them is ill, refuse to let the doctor examine them .He said that he and the other guards just let them get on with it. Their remoteness apart this small group caused no problems for them. "Tell you what Bob, let's stroll up there to have a look at them, see what you think."

Walking through the camp where men were sprawled out on the grass, taking advantage of the warm sun, they were greeted in a friendly manner by the young soldiers, many calling Dicky by name. One wag yelled out, with a grin on his face "Look out its ze gestapo" Robert smiled back and gave the imitation of Nazi salute, which produced a chorus of boos from the relaxing troops. It was all very amicable, and he could see that Dicky and his mates were having a cushy time here. However, as they left the recreation area, and approached the furthest billet, Robert felt a change in atmosphere. Rather ominously the curtains in the hut were drawn, this despite the brightness of the day. Now, as they neared the hut, Robert saw movement at one of the windows, and the curtain was pulled back slightly and a face appeared looking out.

Dicky mounted the three steps to the door and pushed it open. The two men entered to a complete silence, no words of greeting, just blank stares. The men were all seated at a long table on which there were a number of papers which were hurriedly collected up by the sergeant. Dicky greeted them cheerfully and introduced Robert as the local policeman. The already hostile looks became even more pronounced, and the sergeant clumsily rose from his chair, knocking it over in the process. "He has no power here, and we don't want him in our hut" he growled in heavily accented English. From his service in Italy Robert had come to recognise the nuances of the language, and the sergeant's way of speaking did not sound as he thought it should. Dicky ordered the belligerent sergeant to sit down and remember that he was a prisoner of war, and not to address people in such an aggressive manner. However the clearly irritated burly captive was not to change his attitude, and pointing at Robert he screamed "Get out of here, before I hurt you." He then marched towards the two Englishmen, and, pointing to the door, thrust his hand into Robert's chest, and attempted to push him manually out of the hut. Grasping the offending arm the policeman twisted it up behind his attacker's back, and, using the man's own momentum, threw him face down on the floor, still holding the arm in a lock hold, and causing his assailant to scream in agony.

The other prisoners rose as one intent on coming to the aid of their stricken comrade, but froze when Dicky Smith drew his revolver and pointed it threateningly at them. Letting go of the aggressive prisoner, Robert and the guard slowly backed out of the billet with looks of hatred from the inhabitants of the room. Outside a shaken Dicky holstered his gun and said to his companion "I've never known them to be as unfriendly as that before. They're certainly not as friendly and co-operative as the others, but I don't understand why they should react to you in that way." They walked back to Dicky's office and on the way he said "The sooner this place is closed, and the POWs sent home the better. To tell the truth security in here is pretty slack. Every month guards are posted out from here to other duties, and they are often not replaced. Those that are here are not what you'd call frontline soldiers. They're mostly older men who are quite simply waiting to be discharged from the army. Our CO's visits are becoming ever more sporadic, and he rarely inspects the camp, always seeming to have something more important to do. I'll go back to see those churlish men, but don't expect an apology from them." Looking at Robert he said, with a smile "Remind me not to upset you." He had clearly been impressed at the brutal manner in which the policeman, and former soldier, had so easily bested the big sergeant.

Robert left feeling a little unsettled, trying to work out why he had been received in such a malevolent manner, and resolved to inform the inspector of the disturbing event.

CHAPTER ELEVEN

The remainder of the day passed off fairly peacefully. He'd had to hold up the traffic in the village while a flock of sheep was moved from one pasture to another along the lanes. Only Bill ignored his instruction to stop, careering past Robert and racing through the sheep, shepherds and dogs, standing up on his tall bicycle and, as usual inspecting villager's gardens as he wobbled along. The poor shepherd hurled imprecations after the errant cyclist as he collected his scattered ewes together and gently ushered them to their new pasture. That "emergency" dealt with, it was time for Robert to call it a day and go home, but frantic waving from old Maud Brisley caused him to alight from his machine to see what the problem was. Her sister Charlotte had locked herself in a loose box, and was becoming distraught. Using his strength he was able to force the door open and release the tearful old lady. Such a chivalrous act was clearly worth a bottle of Guinness! Robert smiled to himself as he continued on his way. The people of the village, of all ages enriched his life greatly. It was such a peaceful life here in these post war years, and he knew how lucky he was to be able to bring up his little daughter in such a safe and welcoming world. But he could not dismiss the murder from his mind, nor the violence he had so recently encountered at the camp.

Nearly home now he responded to a cheerful wave from Patrick, the former headmaster of the village school. He had taught nearly everybody in the village, and was respected by all. A strict but fair classroom teacher, with a strong right arm when he, on rare occasion had cause to give six of the best to a badly behaved boy. The punishment book showed how infrequently he had had to resort to physical punishment to maintain discipline in the school, preferring to use words rather than the cane. Standing at his garden gate, pipe firmly stuck in his mouth, and snowy white hair cascading over his shoulders, he called out a jaunty greeting to Robert, one of his former pupils. Nowadays the old school master spent his days gardening and walking his old dog. A widower for some time now, with his children living far away, Patrick could be seen most evenings in the Kings Arms, sitting in his favourite corner, pint of beer in one hand, and pipe in the other. He did on occasion imbibe rather too much, but someone would always see that he got home safely. One New Year's Eve Robert had discovered him embracing a bus stop sign and wishing it a Happy New Year. He had escorted the inebriated old man home, and was rewarded with A BOTTLE OF GUINNESS. Was he related to the Brisley sisters?

He was sitting down to read the newspaper after another of Anne's immaculately cooked meals, when the phone rang. It was the duty sergeant at the station urging Robert to report immediately as the inspector wanted to talk to him. The sergeant warned him to be wary as Pengelly was obviously upset over something. Objecting to peremptory commands now that he was no longer a soldier subject to strict discipline, he took his time riding to the station. Greeting his fellow officers in the main office, and noting their worried frowns, he entered the interrogation room where were seated the two London detectives and Inspector Pengelly. The detectives greeted him amicably enough, but the senior officer rewarded him with a furious frown. Barely allowing Robert to sit down he snarled "Just what the hell do you think you are doing Evans? I've had an irate major on the phone this afternoon asking why one of my officers has been interfering with the affairs of a POW camp. You know you have no authority there. That is Ministry of Defence property and is managed only by the army. What on earth persuaded you to go storming in there, and even assaulting one of the inmates?" Annoyed at being spoken to in this manner by Pengelly, Robert answered quietly without raising his voice. "As a matter of course I have always paid a regular visit to the camp, speaking to the duty guard, exchanging pleasantries, having a cup of tea in the guard post, but not venturing further into the restricted area. After all many of the prisoners come into the village and do casual work on the farms. In those circumstances they come under my jurisdiction, and I would be failing in my duty if I just ignored them."

Pointing to the two detectives he went on to say "Our friends here still think our murderer could be someone local, and the prisoners in the camp are as local as are all the people in the area. It was Corporal Smith who invited me in to have a look around, and, for the most part I was welcomed by the men. It was only the inhabitants of one hut who did not welcome my presence, and, as you have no doubt been informed, one of them attacked me. It was completely unprovoked and I did only what was necessary to protect myself without seriously hurting my assailant. Looking towards the London men he said "In view of the slack discipline in the camp where the prisoners appear to come and go as they please, it would be as well to question all of the men there to establish where they were on the night of the murder. Couldn't we ask for help from the MOD police and liaise with them?" While the detectives nodded in agreement, the inspector, still obviously perturbed said to Robert "You will not, under any circumstances go into that camp again, do you understand?" Coldly he replied "perfectly sir, thank you. Is that all sir? With your permission I'll now go about my usual duties, trying not to upset anybody else today." Bidding farewell to the detectives he left the room with head held high. As he rode away from the station to patrol his patch, he was both angry and bemused at the attitude of his superior officer. The failure of the inspector to support his colleague was disappointing and worrying. As far as he was concerned he had done nothing wrong, and certainly did not deserve such a dressing down, especially in front of witnesses. However his greatest concern was for Corporal Dicky Smith, hoping that he too had not got into hot water over his visit to the camp. With that thought in his mind Robert steered his bike towards the prison to see Dicky. Fortunately the corporal was on duty at the gate, and greeted Robert in his usual cheery manner.

The two men now exchanged accounts of their meetings with their superior officers. Dicky reported that his officer had reprimanded him, and warned him not to allow police officers into the camp without his express permission. Remaining outside the gates Robert told him of the furious reaction of Pengelly to the incident in the hut. He asked Dicky to join him that evening, if he was off duty, in the Kings Arms as he wanted to know more of the goings on in the lock-up. The corporal readily agreed to a pint or two in the pub, and the two arranged to meet at eight that evening. Robert now rode off to continue his patrol, with only a tinge of feeling of disloyalty to his inspector and still baffled at his oddball attitude.

Although confident in his ability to handle most problems, he had learnt to rely on his wife Anne, as the person he could talk to when his confidence had taken a knock. So today he decided on an early lunch so that he could tell Anne of the bruising meeting he had had with Inspector Pengelly that morning. Surprised to see her husband, with lunch not yet prepared, nonetheless she greeted him with an affectionate kiss, and immediately put the kettle on. Emily and Meg too fussed around their master, and he rewarded them with hugs before they escaped into the garden to play. Seated at the kitchen table Robert explained exactly what had transpired that morning. He told her of his visit to the camp, of being shown around by the corporal, and of his unexpectedly antagonistic and violent reception in the one hut. He rather glossed over the attack by the prisoner, not wanting to worry Anne. However she instinctively knew that this had been much more serious than he had said. She was aware that there would be times when his job could be dangerous, but she felt confident that he was strong enough and fit enough to deal with any physical problems which might arise. She was also confident that Robert's fellow officers would always back him up when the going got rough, and she was disappointed at the attitude of his inspector.

Robert asked Anne how the villagers felt about the camp and its inhabitants. He had often spoken to the people about this, but always valued her opinion. She knew everybody in the area, and met frequently with the ladies at the church, where she did the flowers for Sunday worship. She would meet daily the parents of the children as they collected their sons and daughters from school. Anne said that, although the huts and wire fences were an eyesore, the men themselves were no problem at all. In fact they were welcomed by most people, being unfailingly friendly and polite, and always willing to help with chores like gardening. She said that the farmers would struggle at haymaking and harvest time without the assistance of the Italians. She smiled as she told him of their attempts to speak English, much to the amusement of the children. "Ciaou" had become a favourite word of the children. Anne concluded by saying that the POWs had given the village extra colour, and most would be sad to see them leave. His wife's observations coincided exactly with his own thoughts on the prisoners, which made the reception of the men in that one hut all the more incomprehensible. As he watched his beautiful wife Robert realised how much he loved her and thought again how lucky he was. He now stood and hugged her long and fiercely, and Emily, running in from the garden, snuggled up to her parents. Not to be left out Meg gave a friendly bark and wagged her tail furiously.

Off once again on his beat noting that the police patrols sent out to reassure people were less frequent now. The occupants of the cars stopped to chat to Robert, more to relieve the boredom of just riding round and round the same streets and lanes. They all reported that they had seen nothing out of the ordinary apart from having to avoid old Bill riding his bike as usual in the middle of the road oblivious to all other road users. However they had been warned about him and studiously ignored his hand gestures as he whipped past them, both hands held aloft in the air with no contact with the handlebars. He was on remote control as ever! The officers in the police cars were from the city and used to more action than they were witnessing here in the countryside. They all said that they were actually enjoying the rural scenery and the serenity of the natural world. When Robert asked them if they wanted to remain down here the answer was a universal "No ta!" He continued his afternoon journey, popping in on Dave Chalmers to ask if he had noticed any strange movement around the big wood or the stand of trees, the site of the killing. With nothing to report he set off for home speeding past the Brisley holding before they could throw another Guinness at him.

CHAPTER TWELVE

That evening when he arrived at the pub there were few customers. The three stalwart cricket spectators, now ostracised from their deck chairs, were playing their usual game of dominoes in the corner. They welcomed Robert only briefly concentrating on their game which to them was more than serious. Enjoying the first taste of his pint of bitter, Robert saw Dicky Smith come in. The corporal was in civvies tonight, casually dressed in an open necked white shirt and black trousers. Robert bought the soldier a pint and the two entered the snug, which was empty of customers, and settled in comfortable armchairs. It was in this room that the committee of the cricket club held their meetings. It was a low-ceilinged nook with old oak beams, and photos of cricket teams, past and present on the whitewashed walls. As secretary of the club, Robert had called many meetings to order in this room. In a corner, in a glass cabinet stood an old bat with a caption that recorded the first century hit on their ground. Next to the exhibit was a photo of the triumphant batsman, cap proudly perched on his head, pint of beer in his hand, and a smile as wide as the sky. Robert had heard talk of the famous sportsman, a gamekeeper by trade, and naturally a poacher in his spare time. His name was Sam Chittenden, and an annual cup for best batting performance was named after him. As was the custom Robert raised his glass to the old warrior before beginning the conversation with Dicky.

The corporal baldly admitted that for him the camp was a cushy number. He said that his basic responsibility was to account for all of the POWs at all times. Nowadays there was a roll call in the evening just before lights out. Each morning after roll call they booked out those who were going out to work on the farms, or simply to explore the countryside. He, together with the other guards, could refuse them from going out if they thought there was no valid reason for so doing, but, Dicky said, he personally had never banned anyone, and the prisoners had always returned to the camp at the allotted time. Like Robert he could report that the local people had no fear of the foreigners, but rather welcomed them. He admitted that the camp was not being run on strict military lines, and all there within the confines of the camp, prisoners and guards alike, were really waiting for the facility to close down so they could all get on with their lives. The CO resented being shunted aside to this little backwater, took little interest in either the POWs or the army personnel looking after them. His visits had become less and less frequent, and of ever shorter duration. He admitted that he could not wait for his retirement from the army, his generous pension, and all the time in the world to play his golf. As a committed regular in the army, Dicky was hoping for a transfer to a training battalion, and had been promised an additional stripe – achieving the same rank as his father before him.

"What about the inimical hut where my visit had caused such an unexpected such a kerfuffle?" asked Robert. Taking a long draught of his beer Dicky said "We don't know much about them really. They were here when I arrived last year. Since they didn't speak the same language as the Italians, they were all put in the same hut together. The big feller who was stupid enough to have a go at you is their leader, and they all seem afraid of him. He's the only one of them who ever leaves the camp, and that only rarely. Where he goes I don't know, except I'm sure he doesn't do any farm work. He never comes back with dishevelled and muddied up clothes like the other farm workers do. Odd thing is that when he signs out and signs back in he always simply puts an "X" whereas the others make proper signatures, even if it's sometimes Benito Mussolini, or Julius Caesar!"

Dicky went on to say that people from that particular hut rarely came out for exercise, and when they did they studiously ignored the other prisoners who tried to engage them in conversation At all muster parades they stay together as a group and answer "si" when their names are called out. He added that, at meal times, one or two of them would go to the mess and collect food for the rest of their people in the hut. "The other POWs call them foreigners, and I think they are a bit afraid of them" said Dicky. "We do, of course, regularly inspect the hut just as we do all of the others, and can find nothing wrong, apart from the frosty reception. If we ask any of them questions, it is always the "boss man" who answers in his guttural, difficult to understand voice. One thing I must say is that their hut is always immaculate, floors polished, bed packs faultlessly made up, and everything spick and span. I don't know which branch of their armed services they served in, but physically they appear very fit, of different heights and build, as you'd expect with a group of twenty men."

"Was there any chance that someone from that hut, or indeed from any of the huts, could have been outside the camp on the evening or night of the murder?" Robert asked his drinking companion. "No chance" replied Dicky. "The camp is locked down at eight pm every day, with everybody who's been out of the camp that day signed back in. We have a roll call each morning after breakfast, and we've never recorded any absentees. That's one thing we are hot on. If we lost someone there'd be hell to pay, and goodbye to my sergeant stripes. There's only one way in and out of the camp unless they can fly, and, in any case, they are all expecting to go home soon anyway, so we don't look for tunnels or other means of escape, what would be the point? Similarly the lure of going home to see family and friends once more means that they obey the rules of the camp without demur."

For both men it had been a convivial evening, and Robert had been given a good idea how the camp was organised. However Dicky's admission that the security of the facility was not perhaps as tight as it should be, left a lingering doubt in his mind about this POW prison stuck here in the middle of the English countryside, and he resolved to investigate further without telling Pengelly of his intentions.

Ironically he was thinking of the inspector when he entered his house later that evening. Anne was waiting for him, a worried look on her face. After greeting her husband with an affectionate kiss, she told him that Pengelly had sent a peremptory message ordering him to report at the station the next morning before beginning his normal duties. He thought "surely he's not going to order me not to associate with the corporal and the camp again". Obviously Anne knew that he had been to the pub to talk to Dicky, and she said indignantly "surely no-one can tell you who you can socialise with can they?" Sitting his wife on his lap and stroking her long fair hair, he said firmly "You know that I will never be bullied by anyone, not even by fast bowlers trying to knock my block off!" this with a big grin. "Don't worry sweetheart, perhaps he's going to commend me for my exemplary work!" They both smiled, and, after looking in on their sleeping daughter cuddling her favourite teddy, they went to bed, and they too drifted off to sleep holding each other close.

The sound of the cockerel from the allotment next door woke them both, and when Emily came in to their bedroom and clambered into their bed, snuggling tightly between them, they all stayed there for some time, warm, cosy and content. Resolutely then Robert rose and went to the kitchen to put on the kettle for the ritual cup of the reviving brew. Then, breakfast over he went to the bathroom for a hands and face wash and a careful shave. A playful session in the garden with Emily and Meg, enjoying the warm early morning sun was followed by a fond farewell as Anne fussed over him checking that his uniform was looking immaculate. Wife and daughter then waved from the garden gate as he rode down the lane and disappeared round the corner on his way to his meeting with his boss. A worried Anne went about her household chores continually looking out of the window to see if her husband had returned. Usually a sensible, well-balanced young woman, she was feeling a little unsettled by the events of the recent past.

Pengelly was alone in the interview room when Robert arrived. He asked the constable to sit, but Robert declined and the two men stood facing one another. Both were tall men, but Robert was perhaps a few inches taller and certainly burlier. Pengelly cleared his throat and spoke "About yesterday, I'm sorry if I was a bit heavy handed in the way I addressed you, but I'd already got it in the neck from the camp CO. I know I haven't been in the area long, but I've been in the job long enough to know we don't interfere in military matters. I've managed to straighten things up with the commandant and assured him that we will confine ourselves to dealing with the prisoners only when they are outside the confines of the camp. There I think we should let the matter rest."

"Would that be all sir?" Robert spoke quietly looking his superior officer in the eye, his face expressionless. It was Pengelly who looked away first as he said "Dismissed". Remembering his military training Robert smartly about turned and marched out of the room. Leaving the station, he mounted his motorbike and set off once again on his daily round. His first stop – the camp where he parked his bike by the gate, and, helmet in hand proceeded to walk purposefully round the perimeter of the prison. He looked to see if there were any breaks in the tall wire fence, or any sign that attempts had been made to burrow under the wire. The ground outside the fences was tall grass, sprinkled with nettles and brambles. There were rabbit holes everywhere, and he thought a chat with Ian Friend about the furry creatures might be worthwhile. There was no sign of men walking through the rough ground. He was only able to walk around about two thirds of the perimeter as the land the furthest from the gates was covered with impenetrable thorn bushes, interspersed with holly and gorse. There was just one lofty ash tree, some fifty yards from the fence, and, as Robert approached it a flock of pigeons, alarmed at his presence, rose as one and soared away towards the large forbidding forest, wings fluttering urgently. He felt the exercise had been worthwhile, and, by not actually going in to the prison, he had not disobeyed Pengelly's instructions.

CHAPTER THIRTEEN

Returning to his bike, he saw a patrol car stationed by the camp gate. His first thought was that Pengelly had followed him, hoping to find him disobeying orders, but stepping out of the car came the two London detectives, Malcolm and Trevor. At the same time the gates opened and Dicky Smith emerged wondering at the arrival of the police car. Re-assured by Robert that there was no problem, the corporal offered them a drink of tea, and he promptly disappeared into the guardroom to emerge shortly with three mugs of the steaming beverage. "Sorry but we don't run to biscuits" Dicky laughingly said and he went back into his post leaving the three policemen to talk. Trevor said how surprised they had been at the inspector's verbal assault on Robert in the station. He added that Pengelly had also been very short with them, and he clearly had some sort of a problem. Robert could not enlighten them saying that he had not known the inspector long. Malcolm informed him that the murder investigation was being scaled down on a local level, and that they now were fairly sure that none of the local people were in any way involved. Patrol cars would continue to drive around the district but less frequently. He and Trevor had been ordered back to London to continue their enquiries from there. They said that no further progress had been made on identifying the victim. Dental records had offered no clue, nor had the clothing in which they found her. The strange "c" in the scar on her back, they felt, was the key to the mystery, but, thus far, even the finest brains at the Met and other crime fighting agencies had not been able to explain its significance. Nonetheless the general feeling was that this was the key which would ultimately unlock the riddle.

Knowing that the detectives were on his side, even if his boss apparently wasn't, put Robert in a happier frame of mind, and he decided to go home now for a mid-morning cup of tea. Arriving there he found his garden occupied by a number of ladies of all ages seated in a circle on the grass animatedly chatting to one another while Emily and her little four legged friend Meg raced around between them using them as a sort of obstacle course. He knew all of these women and they greeted him warmly as Anne rose to kiss him, and Emily ran to him calling "Daddy, daddy!" "We're discussing the village fete, which, if you haven't forgotten, is this Saturday." In truth Robert, with so much on his mind had indeed forgotten all about the annual celebration of the two villages. This festival had a history going back long into the mists of time, and was cancelled only on very rare occasions. During the war of course, with aeroplanes wheeling about in the skies trying desperately to shoot each other down, and lone German raiders strafing anything which moved, it would have been foolish to gather together in large numbers. In the summer of 1944 people began to feel a little safer, and a small fete was held, but when a doodlebug clattered over the village, panic set in and everybody rushed for shelter. Now that the hostilities were thankfully over, the age old tradition could once again re-commence.

The fete was shared by the two villages. This year was Elwood's turn to host the event, and all that week there was feverish activity to make this the best ever celebration, despite the constraints of rationing. It was, of course the ladies of the villages who led the preparations. The members of the Women's' Institute took the lead in decorating the village hall, with banners and streamers, inside and out. It was in the hall that the jumble sale would be held, stalls manned by the members, and it was here that prizes would be presented. On the field behind the hall members of the cricket club laid out markers for the various events which would take place on the closely cut grass. Robert noted that even Ian Friend had helped out, an unlikely smile on his face. Sceptics might say that it was because he was expecting to win many of the sporting events to be held there. All through the village flags and other bunting began to appear on the cottages and on the school, and a great, if slightly tatty union jack festooned the front of the Kings Arms. There was frenzied activity in the steeple of the church where efforts were being made by the mechanics from the local garage to try to persuade the bells to ring out once again. During the war years they had only been rung to warn of invasion. The bell-ringers, inactive for so long, could barely wait to show off their expertise in the art of campanology.

During the remainder of that week there was an air of expectancy throughout the two settlements. The children especially excitedly awaiting the great day. Behind closed doors parents and their off springs made ready, preparing food, looking out their best, Sunday clothes, and some sewing and knitting outfits for the fancy dress. The fete was just the boost needed to raise the spirits of the two communities after the shocking discovery of the dead girl in the wood.

Robert had continued with his daily routine, assisting with the preparations for the festivities in the evenings together with Anne and Emily, as ever accompanied by her faithful Meg. After working in the sports field, they would adjourn to the pub where they would sit in the pub garden, eating crisps and drinking beer. Emily felt all grown up as she sat at the table with mum and dad sipping her Tizer through a straw. Then a stroll through the village enjoying the soft evening summer air redolent with scents of the countryside, and listening to the birds whistling their goodnight tunes, the sheep baaing in the meadow, and the mournful lowing of Dave Chalmers' cattle. As the light began to fade bats emerged flitting about with boundless energy seeking their evening food.

The gods smiled on the people of Elwood that Saturday. The morning sun rose behind the Oak Hill forest and cast long shadows over the village. Everybody rose early on this special day. The expectation was beyond high. Today the war years, the rationing, and the recent murder could all be put behind them, and they could enjoy themselves once again. However they were not to know on this bright , promising summer day that yet another calamity was about to befall them.

In the Evans household there was great excitement, largely coming from Emily. An excitement equally shared by Meg. The little girl was to be a contestant in the fancy dress competition, and could not wait for mum to put on her costume as Little Red Riding Hood, with Meg, perhaps a bit unfairly as the Big Bad Wolf. Robert's playful suggestion that Anne should be the old granny was met with a hefty smack on her husband's back. Since the gala would not open until the afternoon, the Evans went for a long walk to the Chalmers' farm where Emily could see the animals, and climb in the barn with its sweet smelling bales of hay, looking for hens' eggs and the nests of swallows in the eaves. If Robert and Anne thought that their daughter would be tired after the expedition they were sadly mistaken and, as soon as they arrived home, Emily was demanding "When can we go to the fair please?"

At last, lunch over, they set off for the fair, Emily and Meg in their fancy dress now while dad wore his best police uniform. This was not through choice but was at the insistence of the organising committee who wanted to see their "Bobby", feeling that, in the excitement of the day, he would provide a calming influence should anyone become too boisterous. The firemen from the neighbouring town were there too, together with their formidable fire engine, and there were uniformed nurses from the cottage hospital, St John's ambulance folk, and, of course scouts, guides and brownies, all with their leaders. It all added to the pageantry of the occasion. Having escorted his family to the fete, Robert now returned home to fetch his motorcycle, knowing that the children would want to sit on the machine, and try on his helmet.

Promptly at one o'clock the chairman of the parish council, Mister Claude Pincher, accompanied by his wife Audrey, cleared his throat and, standing on the steps in front of the village hall began to make the requisite speech which would set the activities in motion. Smiling benignly at his expectant audience, resplendent in his best black three piece suit, watch chain dangling over his ample paunch and spectacles perched on the end of his bulbous nose, he began "Ladies and gentlemen" some wag in the crowd yelled "What about the others?" which brought cackles from his unruly friends. A stern look from Robert was enough to prevent any more heckling. The speech was, thankfully not a long one, and would have been even shorter but for the councillor's unfortunate stutter.

Official business completed, the fun could now start. On the field the competitions began. First the races, the sack race which caused much hilarity as most of the competitors fell at least once, before the vicar, the Reverend Harris, eventually stumbled over the line to win the rosette. There were disqualifications in this event as some enterprising entrants had surreptitiously cut holes in the corners of their bags. Next the three-legged race where co-ordination was the key to success, but, of the ten contestants, only one couple managed to "co-ordinate" sufficiently well to complete the course. The losing competitors were sprawled at various parts of the track, mostly convulsed with laughter, totally unworried at their undignified poses. For the egg and spoon race entrants had to produce their own eggs owing to rationing. This event was for children of eight or under, and the be whiskered old gentleman who appeared at the starting line equipped with a soup ladle and goose egg was promptly disqualified midst peals of laughter. There were a number of sprint races for children, boys and girls of different ages, encouraged raucously by admiring parents, and a race for mums and dads, with Anne winning her event easily, as Emily squealed her to the winning post. Robert resisted demands that he entered the race, knowing that, wearing his heavy boots, he stood no chance of competing with the likes of Ian Friend, and the other cricketers.

The tug of war between teams from the two villagers lasted for many minutes with the sides evenly matched. Eventually the Elwood men managed to drag their opponents over the specified mark, whereby both teams collapsed with exhaustion, before shaking hands with their adversaries, and staggering off to the hall for alcoholic refreshments. The slow bicycle "race", by its very nature, lasted even longer, and the few spectators watching it soon gave up, not really caring by now who was actually victorious. Tossing the large bag of hay over the bar was won predictably by Dave Chalmers who didn't even need to take off his jacket to triumph over all the other strong men. His opponents suggested, laughingly, that he had put lead weights in their particular bags.

Although there was no cricket match today, the cricketers were all eager to show off their prowess with the ball, and it was that demon fast bowlers Ian Friend who demonstrated the strength of his bowling arm by hurling the little red ball a prodigious distance, yards further than his opponents. Robert was content to watch this contest, but was not persuaded to enter it. However Anne and Emily insisted that he had a go at the welly whanging, and he managed to hurl the number eleven rubber boot much further than anyone else. Unfortunately his missile finished up in the nearby field startling the sheep peacefully grazing there, and his effort was ruled a no throw.

The animals entered for the dog show were remarkably well behaved, unlike last year when there was a mass snarling, and the judge, the local vet received a nasty nip on his calf. The pets were judged, not merely by their well-groomed appearance and behaviour, but the demeanour of their handlers. Anne had decided not to enter Meg and Emily in this event, but of course the winner could not hold a candle to the little girl's own dog. Because of the fine weather, the fancy dress competition would be held on the field once the sporting activities had been completed. There was great interest in the parade as the entrants walked elegantly round under the eyes of the judges, all of whom were members of the parish council. The costumes, all handmade, brought rounds of applause from the attentive onlookers, amazed at the skill and inventiveness of the makers of the clothes. There was much deliberation by the arbiters, but eventually rosettes were awarded to the three competitors considered to be the best. Emily was happy to be congratulated on her costume, and hugged Meg in delight.

Stalls had been arranged around the edge of the field, and were attracting much interest. A limited amount of food was on sale, with the ice cream seller doing a roaring trade. Sandwiches and cakes too were very popular, as were bottles of lemonade, and other fizzy drinks. For the adults the landlord of the Kings Arms had set up a bar where beer, cider and shandy were being consumed by the thirsty patrons. Inside the hall any manner of things, but mostly clothing had been laid out on tables for the jumble sale. Perhaps unsurprisingly there a number of gas masks for sale, and these were eagerly snapped up to be kept as a souvenir of the bad times. Robert wondered if these items should have been handed in, but it was a nice day and he had no desire to offend people. The stalls were manned by the members of the WI, who were also dispensing cups of tea, with just one biscuit per customer and that a plain one. Raffle tickets were on sale here with the most coveted prize being a large box of chocolates. All of the prizes had been donated by members of the public. With the day coming to an end, the chairman announced that a substantial amount had been raised for the village hall fund, and he thanked all of the people who had made the day such a success, and he thanked everyone for coming. The vicar then delivered a short prayer of thanks, and the day culminated with three hearty cheers for the chairman of the council.

CHAPTER FOURTEEN

The partygoers gathered together their children, dogs and belongings while stall holders and organisers began to dismantle their stands and take away any unsold goods. The field was rapidly being swept clear of all of the paraphernalia of the fair, and reverting to its normal pristine state, if looking a little trampled by the many feet bruising the grass. The air of business-like bustle, conducted in a quiet manner was then shattered by the violent and noisy invasion of a clearly agitated Silly Bill, riding his old bicycle into the meadow at great speed, and yelling something quite unintelligible. This was perhaps the most chilling aspect of his intrusion, for Bill had not spoken for years. He was riding from person to person, obviously looking for someone, a look of abject horror on his face, pointing with great agitation in the direction of his cottage.

Catching sight of Robert, Bill raced furiously to the policeman, waving his arms about and mouthing words. Frightened by the look on Bill's face, and the fact that he was obviously deeply troubled by something, everybody stood still, silent and bewildered. Some of the younger children began to cry, clinging on to their parents. They all had the same look on their faces as they had when first hearing and seeing the doodlebugs roaring through the skies above them. Instinctively they all looked to Robert for re-assurance.

Bill had dismounted from his bike and was pulling Robert's arm, dragging him towards his motorbike, all the while trying to tell the policeman what the problem was. He had never seen the old man so agitated and allowed himself to go with him. Bill then pointed in the direction of his cottage, and, mounting his bike once again set off, as usual at a great rate of knots. In a commanding voice, Robert told everybody to remain where they were and to stay calm, while he went to see what had so panicked the old man. Without bothering to put on his helmet, he then set off after him along the lane which led to Liz's dwelling. Ian Friend too grabbed one of the bikes from a competitor in the slow bike race, and, pedalling furiously set off after the two escapees. A worried Anne, holding Emily's hand watched her husband until he disappeared down the lane, and, like everybody else wondered what had so disturbed the old soldier. Reaching his house Bill got off his trusty steed and, with a stumbling run, set off through his garden, through the hedge at the bottom, and, waving at Robert to follow him, now ran, weaving from side to side, across the hay meadow towards the stand of trees which bordered the field. Ian and Robert raced after him, and caught him up at the edge of the wood. As they raced past the cottage, Liz appeared, alarmed at the frenzied activity, and completely unaware of what had happened. Not being at ease with crowds of people, she has not gone to the fair but had generously donated articles of clothing she had fashioned herself on her old loom. She now watched in amazement as her brother, hotly pursued by Robert and Ian.

Together the trio, transport put aside with Bill in the lead, entered the trees, brushing aside the thorn bushes which barred their passage. Some twenty yards in, at the foot of a large ash tree, Bill pointed to the ground, and, partially hidden by small branches and twigs which had been strewn over her, was the body of a young woman. The three men stood there in those beautiful surroundings gazing with horror at the appalling and tragic sight before their eyes. Ian's face was ashen, and tears were streaming down Bill's face. Robert shook himself and his police, and army training kicked in. Turning to the young poacher he barked "Ian, go to the phone box and tell them that I need support. Say nothing to the people, but stay there to direct my colleagues to this spot." Ian looked once more at the body on the ground, to assure himself that this was real, before running off to do as the officer had demanded of him. Old Bill stood hunched over rubbing his hands together incessantly, and Robert knew that he must jerk the old man out of his misery. "Bill," he said," I want to thank you for what you've done today. You should be immensely proud of yourself. Now I want you to go home to your sister. " At these words of commendation, the first he had received since his days in the trenches, the old warrior Bill drew himself up to attention and threw his hand up in an immaculate salute, smiled at Robert and turned to leave the scene of the tragedy, and to go home to be comforted by his sister. As he entered the garden, Liz could see the distress on his face and put her arms around him and led him into their cottage. She was, of course fully aware that he could not tell her what had happened, but she knew that she would find out later.

Alone Robert stood looking down at the forlorn looking body, lying on her back on the floor of the wood. She looked to be perhaps in her twenties, tall, slim of build, fair of hair, wearing a blue dress, but with nothing on her feet. A small nose, regular features and wide open blue eyes, she was very pretty. The only ugliness about her was the knife sticking out from her breast, and the blood which had flowed from that ghastly wound. Robert shivered and he somehow had a premonition that, when she was turned over, a hideous scar would be seen on her back. Sadly he thought that, at least, there was no cricket ball involved this time.

Pengelly not being on duty, it was an inspector from a neighbouring town who arrived with Ian. He was accompanied by two uniformed constables. All three were known to Robert. Thanking Ian for his support, he asked him to tell his Anne that he would be busy for a while yet, but that he was alright, and would explain later. The officers now began to process the scene carefully without disturbing any evidence. The inspector, a bluff Yorkshire man called Roland lit a cigarette and said to Robert "What sort of a mess have you got here Bob? This used to be a nice quiet area, now you've produced two murders in as many weeks. Is there something different in the water nowadays?" Brusquely he then directed one of the officers carefully to look around to see if there was anything suspicious which would merit further immediate investigation. The other constable was ordered to send for the forensic team, and the support of other policemen to seal off the scene.

The prof arrived some thirty minutes later, dishevelled as ever and puffing mightily as he fought his way through the foliage to reach the scene of the crime. Eyeing Robert he said "Are you attracting these bodies constable. You're becoming like a moth to a flame." Then, like the true professional he was, he began to examine the whole scene around the body, even scrutinising the leaves and branches of the trees casting ever moving shadows as they swayed and danced with the breeze. Having satisfied himself with his survey, he asked Robert to assist him in turning the corpse over, equipping him with surgical gloves beforehand. Gently they rolled the girl over, with the prof noting that rigor mortis had not yet fully set in. Both immediately marked the, now familiar ugly scar burned crudely into the skin of the lady's back. Again it appeared that an attempt had been made to disguise what was under the scar. The disfigurement was about the same length as the previous one, but, this time the last letter or symbol was only just visible, and seemed to be the letter "P". Shaking his head the prof asserted "Looks like another one for the boffins doesn't it." Inspector Roland asked if the scientist could give them any information right now about the murder. The prof mused for a moment and then said "Looks like the same killer or killers. Death must have been instantaneous. I would say time of death was probably early this morning, but I can tell you more when I've got the poor lass on my slab." With that he directed the body to be removed, and, shaking hands with Robert and the inspector, he left to return to his laboratory.

Roland told Robert that he and his men would take care of securing the scene, and he told Robert to go home, knowing that his wife would be worried about him, and would want to know what had caused Bill to be so upset. First he went to Bill's dwelling where he found the old man much calmer. He told Liz what had happened, and her brother's discovery of the body, and how he had led Robert to the scene. He assured her that Bill was not in any sort of trouble, but that he should remain at home for a while because, once the newspapers had got wind of the murder, they would be eager to interview him, unaware that he could not speak. He didn't want the old fellow to be upset again. He then left the old couple and went home. The officers who had accompanied Inspector Roland told the people still at the fete that a body had been found, but gave no details. They asked the villagers to go home, and that officers would be talking to them soon. The inspector asked who had telephoned the police, and made a point of thanking Ian which gave the young man a surprising amount of pleasure.

Having told Anne of the events of that memorable day which had started so encouragingly, had given so much pleasure and fun, but had then ended so tragically. News of the death had spread rapidly through the village and people were stunned. They had not yet completely got over the first death and now here was another. Rumours and speculation were, of course, rife. All sorts of wild theories were being bandied about. Was this another Jack the Ripper? Who would be next? Was it someone who just hated young women? Parents would keep a close eye on their daughters, forbidding them to go out alone in the evening. Fortunately they knew nothing about the scars, for that knowledge would have greatly increased their anxiety. Robert told Anne that Inspector Roland had taken over the investigation until the murder squad detectives could return to the village and assume command once more. Relieved to hear that her husband was not needed any more today, she hugged him, and told him to lock the door and ignore any visitors who might come seeking information about the events of the day. Thus they could spend a peaceful evening listening to the radio and enjoying a glass of wine which they had been saving for Anne's birthday.

That Saturday then passed into history, a day which would stay in the memory for years to come. Twenty four short hours of twists and turns, of hope enjoyment and despair, of ups and downs. As Robert drifted off to sleep, his dreams were tormented by the vision of the pretty young woman, slaughtered midst the beauty of the trees, displaying all of their summer finery, mute witnesses to the murder. He knew that the next few days and weeks would be demanding ones and he thanked the Lord for giving him such a loving family to support him as he carried out his duties. These were his first murders and he prayed that he would not let himself down in any way.

CHAPTER FIFTEEN

Sunday morning brought frequent showers of warm rain, and it was Anne who took Meg for her early walk, leaving Emily to supervise her dad preparing the vegetables for lunch. Out of the kitchen window he could see a stream of passers-by, all peering curiously at him and waving, with a nagging itch to question him about the death in the wood, but regretfully continuing on their way. An exasperated Anne returned having herself been pestered for news, and relieved to enter the house and firmly shut the door. Closing the curtain of the kitchen window the couple sat down to peruse the Sunday newspapers. As usual Robert turned first to the sports pages to check the county cricket scores, pleased as Punch when he saw that his hero Trevor Bailey had excelled once again with bat and ball, and he looked forward to seeing that man's name on the team sheet for the forthcoming test match against India. Anne was encouraged to see that some of the rationing was now being relaxed, and at mealtimes she would soon be able to serve up a greater variety of food. It was too soon for news of the murder to be reported, but Robert had visions of hordes of reporters descending on the village in the next few days. Ruefully he thought that the proprietor of the Kings Arms would be licking his lips at the prospect of all of these thirsty city folk coming through his doors. "It's an ill wind" he muttered to himself.

Anne was just laying the table for the mid-day meal when there was a frantic knocking on the door. With Meg barking furiously Robert went to open, only to find a distraught Liz, tears streaming down her face, standing there, trying to tell him something. It was Anne who led her in to the kitchen, sat her down and made her a cup of tea. Then, holding the old lady's hand, she asked her what on earth was the matter. Looking at Robert the distraught old lady blurted out "They've arrested my Bill, and put him in a prison cell. Please Mister Evans, you must help us." Tell us exactly what happened Liz" Robert gently asked her. Holding her cup with trembling hands, she explained in a voice only just above a whisper "It was that Inspector Pengelly who came banging on my door. There were two other officers with him. He was right nasty, barging his way into the house without a by your leave". "Where's that daft brother of yours" he shouted, and marched into my living room where my Bill was sitting. "Arrest him" Pengelly instructed one of the policemen, "and put him in cuffs". Bill, of course couldn't protest, and offered no resistance when the handcuffs were put on his wrists. He just looked totally confused, but, as he was led away, he stood up straight and looking fiercely at his sister almost marched out of the house." When I asked where they were taking him, I was told "to the police station" and, without a word of explanation they put my brother in the back of their car and left. Robert asked her if they had actually cautioned Bill, but Liz shook her head, saying that she had no idea what it was all about and she didn't understand the meaning of a caution.

He asked Liz to stay with Anne for a while and he went to put on his uniform. As he dressed he became more and more angry at the way the old soldier had been treated, and he was puzzled at the behaviour of the inspector. Returning to the two ladies he told them that he would go immediately to the station to find out what was going on. When Anne protested that he had not yet eaten his lunch, he said, with a smile "I'm sure Liz is hungry, and can eat my lunch. I'll be back as soon as I can, hopefully with Bill as well." With that he mounted his motorcycle and sped off for the police station.

Dismounting from his bike, Robert took a few minutes to compose himself. He was coldly angry at the way the old man, a soldier who had suffered severely because of his experiences in the Great War, had been treated, and was determined to discover why the harmless veteran had been arrested. Entering the station he could see that he was expected. The desk sergeant Arthur Vile was an old copper, well versed in the ways of the service. He had known Robert for a long time, and respected him for his fairness and sound judgement. "What's going on sarge?" he asked of his old colleague. "Pengelly's told us nothing" replied Arthur. "He just dragged old Bill in here, told me to book him in, and then marched him to the cells. He then cleared off home, saying he would deal with it in the morning. I've taken Bill some sandwiches and a drink, and I'm keeping an eye on him. We all feel sorry for him stuck in that cell, looking completely lost." Arthur admitted that no attempt had been made to get legal representation for the prisoner, and Robert asked if he would be allowed to go and see him. The desk sergeant hesitated for a moment before handing over the keys to the cell, and warning him not to be too long.

Bill was the sole prisoner in the cells that Sunday morning. He looked up bewildered when he heard the heavy keys rattle in the lock, but, when he saw Robert enter he stood up, heels together, at attention, and saluted his welcome visitor. He was once again the proud old soldier, and this was his honoured officer. The two men sat on the sparse bed and an inevitable one-sided conversation took place. Bill may not have been able to talk, but he was not stupid, and Robert was sure that he would understand what he told him. "I'm going to get you out of here Bill," he began. "I know, in fact everyone knows, that you have done nothing wrong. I can't figure out why you are in here, but I certainly will find out. I'll have to ask you to be patient until I can get you released. Be assured that Anne and I will see that your sister is ok, and Sergeant Vile will look after you while you're here". He got up to leave and Bill rose with him, smiled and grasped his hand with a firm handshake which lasted for some time. Robert was humbled by the trust which Bill had in him and feared what the future might have for him. He left Bill lying on the Spartan bed in that small, bleak room, and shook his head in despair.

Returning to the front office to hand in the keys, he was surprised to see Inspector Pengelly enter. Seeing the keys in Robert's hand he snarled "Just what the hell do you think you are doing with those constable?" "Determined not to be bullied or intimidated by his superior officer, he said in a calm, but firm voice "I've just been to see an old friend of mine who has been stuck in a tiny cell for some obscure reason which I cannot fathom." The inspector's face reddened and his eyes bulged as he blurted out "Are you questioning my authority and judgment Evans, if so you had better be very careful." Again Robert's reply was measured and he retorted. "Bill is a member of the community for which I have had responsibility for a number of years, and I surely have the right to ask why he has been arrested. I must also question why he has not been cautioned, nor told on what charge he is being held. Why has he not been given legal representation?"

In a menacing voice Pengelly demanded "Who gave you permission to interview my prisoner in the cell? You know that is a disciplinary matter". As he said this he glared at Sergeant Vile saying "I'll deal with you later Vile " Looking directly at his accuser, Arthur said, with great dignity, "You may be of higher rank than me, but you will address me as Sergeant Vile sir." The inspector pointed an aggressive finger at the sergeant, thought about saying something, but turned his attention to Robert. "You will apologise to me, and to Sergeant Vile for your breach of procedure". The sergeant, deeply offended by his superior's contemptuous attitude told him that any breaking of the rules was down to him, as the officer responsible for prisoners, and he accepted being out of order. Coldly Robert stated "I surely owe the sergeant an apology for causing him so much bother, but I have no intention whatever of apologising to you. Your bullying and hectoring manner to us both is totally unacceptable and unprofessional and I intend to report it to the superintendent. Neither Sergeant Vile or I have done anything that merits such high-handed treatment from a fellow officer."

Pengelly took a step towards Robert, and Arthur, figuring that the verbal interplay might become physical, came from behind his desk ready to intervene. However Robert, impassive of face, stood his ground, hands by his side, unthreatening. Still in the mistaken belief that he could make the officer back down, the inspector now launched into a tirade of abuse, mostly in English, but also in a strange language which Robert assumed to be his native Welsh. Aware that his bluster was having no effect on Robert, Pengelly took a step back and paused, while Robert stood, feet together, stony-faced. The inspector then intoned "You are suspended from duty as of this moment. Hand over your warrant card to the sergeant" At these savage words both officers looked shocked, but, without demur, Robert reached in to his tunic, pulled out the card, and laid it on the desk. Pointing to the card which had meant so much to Robert for so long, the inspector said "And the keys to your machine." These were placed carefully beside the warrant card, and, looking straight in to Pengelly's eyes, he breathed "Do you want my uniform as well sir?" "Just get out" growled the inspector, and Robert, bidding farewell to Arthur, left the station without a look backward.

It was a walk of more than five miles to Elwood. The first two miles was through the suburbs of the town. The going was easy, being for the most part flat, on well-maintained pavements, with, thankfully little signs of dog muck and only the occasional piece of litter. Now, with time on his hands, and not speeding through the town on his motorbike, he could appreciate the houses and bungalows which lined his route. He was impressed with the colourful front gardens with their flower borders and small ornamental trees, dreaming in the summer sun. There were very few cars on this Sunday morning, and only one green and white bus, with just the uniformed driver on board, drove slowly past him, giving him a cheerful if puzzled wave as he went. Robert realised that he must present an unusual sight sporting a crash helmet and gauntlets but missing a bike. Reaching the edge of the town there were more trees on the pavement, for which he was increasingly grateful as he was by now perspiring freely in his heavy uniform. The sun was almost at its zenith, and the heat was growing.

He soon approached the parish church, with its huge tower and ancient clock. The clock was in need of repair, if repair was possible. It always showed the same time, and Robert was reminded of old Bill, sitting forlornly in his lonely prison cell and his fixation on a particular time. There were more people now, members of the congregation on their way to the morning service. Robert noticed how smart they looked, the men in their three-piece suits, mostly black or dark grey, roses creating a splash of colour in their lapels. With boots which shined reflecting the sun, and trilbies or flat caps perched smartly on their heads, Robert wondered whether they were all ex-servicemen, or did they have wives who checked their appearance before letting them out in the public gaze? On the arms of the military looking men were their wives dressed in their Sunday finery, long summery gowns, no make-up, but a variety of hats, which drew envious or disdainful looks from the other ladies. The children too were all smartly turned out, the boys with their short trousers and smarmed down hair, and the girls in summer dresses and pretty little bonnet. Clothes rationing clearly did not prevent them from putting on a show. At the church door stood the vicar, bible in hand, greeting the faithful members of his flock. Wistfully Robert recalled his childhood and the Sunday mornings he had gone to St. Michaels in the village, and had sat for what seemed an interminably long time as the service was conducted. He remembered all of the familiar hymns and had actually enjoyed singing along with his family and friends. To him as a young lad the sermons seemed pointless and almost endless. He vividly recalled his dad nudging him when he fidgeted. One Christmas the vicar had announced that he had a sore throat, and Robert cheered inwardly expecting a shorter lecture, only to be disappointed as the man of God droned on even longer than usual.

Leaving the pavements of the town behind him, the now suspended officer strode out purposefully along the familiar lanes which would take him home. Walking allowed him the time to appreciate the glory of the summer landscape, and to hear the songbirds trilling in the trees. He whistled back to them, thanking them for lifting his spirits. He thanked the trees swaying way above his head for providing shade from the sun shining down from the blue, cloudless sky. He thought that, hot it might be, but much preferable to having to undertake this trek in the pouring rain. In his mind he ran over the events of the morning, of the sight of poor Bill, lonely and bewildered in the confines of his cell. This was a man for the freedom of the woods, the meadows, the stream and the woods, not for being pent up in a tiny space with bare walls, and one small window from which he could see only another wall. Robert reflected that the old man was infinitely worse off than the Italian POWs who at least could leave their quarters for some time if they so wished.

CHAPTER SIXTEEN

Heartened by the sight of the church spire in the village, he quickened his step, ignoring his parched throat and aching feet. There had been no traffic along the country lanes so far, but then he heard the sound of a tractor, trundling along behind him. He was elated to see that it was Dave Chalmers driving the noisy, smelly beast, pulling a trailer with a few bales of hay on it. He stopped alongside Robert and mockingly asked "Has that little pop-pop of yours broken down officer?", "Are you licensed to carry passengers on that dirty old contraption?" Robert replied with a relieved grin, and he scrambled aboard, sitting at the front on a hay bale on the wooden trailer, and leaning over to talk to his Good Samaritan. As they set off he said to the farmer "You may not believe this but I've been suspended from duty, so you don't need to worry about all those illegal activities you carry out on the farm." The two friends laughed, but then Dave, speaking loudly over the noise of the Fordson engine, said "Hey this is ridiculous, Bob, they can't suspend you. We all, except maybe Ian Friend, rely on you and trust you. Perhaps I should go and have a word with your bosses to put them straight on a few things." Robert smiled and replied "Well at least I can have a bit of a holiday, until my fate is decided by the powers that be". "To hell with that" retorted Dave "if you think you're going to sit on your arse at home doing nothing all day, you can think again. As of today you are my cowman and shepherd. You can start by doing the milking this afternoon Robert accepted the offer of employment eagerly. He would put all of his energy into the post of farm labourer, and looked forward to working with the cattle, horses and sheep on Dale's farm.

Driving through the village at the pedestrian pace of the tractor, Robert's appearance, seated on the trailer, attracted many a surprised look, and a few derisory comments, with people thinking that his trusty steed had broken down. However he knew that news of his suspension would soon spread throughout the community, and he could expect many visitors, most of them he hoped supportive.

Most surprised of all were Anne and Emily as the tractor pulled up at their gate and Robert, crash helmet in hand, leapt off, thanking Dave and promising not to be late for the milking. Now to tell his wife what had happened at the station, and the reason for his unusual form of transport. Cold drinks in hand the little family adjourned to the garden where they sat in the shade, sheltered from the near tropical heat of the sun. Before he began his discourse Robert was silent for a while drinking in the beauty of his surroundings. He mused "I've the best, prettiest wife in the whole world, the most wonderful daughter, the most affectionate little dog, and, raising his head he bellowed "The best life any man could have!" The two ladies in his life embraced him tenderly, and Meg wagged her tail so furiously that she almost took off! From the ash tree at the back of their cottage a flock of pigeons frantically took off, desperately trying to escape from the sudden noise.

They sat there for a long while in a companiable silence, enjoying the peace of the afternoon, while Emily, happily sucking her thumb, curled up on her mother's lap and drifted off to sleep. Meg too decided to join in and, lying on Robert's feet, succumbed to the warmth and slept. Anne could hardly contain herself, desperate to know the reason for Robert's arrival by tractor. Her first thought was that the police vehicle had broken down, but that did not explain his euphoric behaviour on seeing her and Emily.

He then told her, blow by blow of the events at the station, of his seeing Bill in that cell, and of Pengelly's unreasonable and unprofessional fury when he entered the station and learnt of his talking to the old man. Anne was horrified to hear of the bullying manner in which he had treated Robert and Sergeant Vile. Arthur Vile's wife was a good friend and Anne knew that she too would be angry at the way in which her husband had been treated. Robert said that technically the inspector had every right to chastise him, but to suspend him was going too far. He could not understand his superior's antagonism to him, and felt that he was becoming increasingly irrational. "However," he told Anne, "as of this moment I am an ex-copper, and am now a full-time cowman, working for Dave Chalmers." Shocked Anne replied "you can't surely leave it at that. You are an excellent policeman with an unblemished record. They can't simply discard you like that." Kissing her on the cheek Robert said "tomorrow, Monday I'll get in touch with my federation and ask for their help. My first and most pressing concern is Bill. I'll get in touch with Brian, he's a solicitor, and I'll ask him to represent him, difficult though it may be with Bill unable to speak". They decided that, once Emily was awake they would go to see Liz to offer her their support. Robert had no logical explanation to give her as to why her brother had been arrested, but he would tell her that he was finding a solicitor to support him.

As they strolled back from Liz's cottage accompanied by a now awake Emily and Meg, Anne wondered how they could best help the old couple. Their parents had both been farm workers, not educated to any acceptable standard, and living the life of all rural folk, hardworking and honest with little interest in what went on beyond the confines of their village community. With brother Bill going off to fight in a war of which they had not the slightest knowledge, it was left to Liz to look after her now ageing parents. When their shell-shocked son returned they had great difficulty coming to terms with his mental state. This was not the big strong son they remembered, who had gladly left to serve his country, not the warrior home on leave in his smart khaki uniform. He was now a shadow of his former self, gaunt, with thinning hair, and uncommunicative. They were unable to comprehend the explanation the doctor gave them for his condition, and felt that it would only be time before he was their own Billy once again. As the years passed they came to accept that he would always be the damaged man that he had become, and, as they became more and more senile, the burden fell on Liz to nurse her family. The parents dead, brother and sister continued with their simple way of life, both increasingly reliant on each other, and accepting their lot with stoical acceptance.

On their way back home, Anne suddenly stopped mid-stride, and, grasping Robert's arm, blurted out "I know what we can do. We can take Bill's bike to the garage and get the mechanics to give it a good service. At the very least we can get a new saddle fitted, the one that's on it must give him a sore bum. And new tyres, and mudguards, perhaps even some lights, and a bell one with a really loud ring so we can hear him coming and get out of his way. Then we can paint the frame." Robert laughed out loud at the sheer enthusiasm in Anne's voice and agreed whole-heartedly, saying that tomorrow he would wheel the machine to the garage and talk to the owner.

CHAPTER SEVENTEEN

That afternoon, dressed in his "farming" clothes, green overall, flat cap and sturdy boots Robert duly walked to the Chalmers' farm, greeted Dave and his wife, and, stick in hand, walked out to the big hay meadow to call the cows in for milking. They all knew his voice, since he had worked with them many times, and they wandered in in that relaxed way that only bovines could muster, towards the open gate which would lead them to the cowshed. As always big Tiny was the boss cow leading her minions, and, bringing up the rear came dear old Dolly, like an abstracted old professor, mind as ever miles away. Tying the animals up in their stalls the ex-policeman could forget about all of his problems as he talked to the huge, docile cattle, and prepared the machines for milking. He thought that it wasn't long ago when he, like many dairymen before, him would have been sitting on a three-legged stool, bucket between his knees, and using his hands to extract the milk and hearing the comforting sound of the precious liquid hitting the bottom of the bucket.

The day's milk cooled and poured safely into the churns, it was now time to unchain the cows and follow them as they made their amiable way back to the meadow where they could methodically munch the nourishing grass, and enjoy the slowly fading sun on their backs. Next washing the milking equipment and walking to the farmhouse to chat with Dave and his wife. This couple were two of his oldest friends and, after his wife, were people on whom he could always rely for support and advice. As Dave's wife Julie poured the tea, she said "If you're going to talk cricket, I'll go and feed the hens." However, important as the great game was to both of the men, there were more pressing things to discuss.

Robert told his friend that he would, of course, be disputing his suspension, and would be consulting with his federation. He also told him that he was arranging for Bill to be legally represented, and of the plan to service his old bicycle .Dave applauded him for these initiatives, and offered to help in any way he could. Robert then pledged to procure Bill's release by investigating the two murders himself and bringing to justice the actual murderer, or murderers He acknowledged that he was not trained in detective work, but would use his own l knowledge to try to discover the truth. He said that, although in his opinion, nobody in the locality would be capable of such callous brutality, nonetheless there must surely be some local connection. He said that, whenever his agricultural commitments would allow, he intended to speak to everyone in the two villages, not forgetting the farmers and their employees. At Dave's offer of a tractor to make him mobile, Robert laughed and said that he would get his trusty old bike from the shed, and use that as his transport. It was the same bike he had ridden a few years past when he delivered papers each morning before going to school.

He then returned home carrying a bottle of fresh milk, and a dozen newly-laid eggs which Julie had thrust upon him as he left the Chalmers' farm. He now told Anne what he had told Dave, of his plans for the immediate future, and she hugged him, loving him for not becoming depressed at his turn of fortunes, but rather looking forwards with a determination to put things right once again. She had every confidence that he would succeed.

Monday morning, bike tyres pumped up, and saddle adjusted to his now taller stature, he set off through a drenching rain to see to his cows. As he rode he thought that the rain would do the cricket square good, as they had experienced a dry spell of late. This morning he had almost finished milking when Dolly, in a world of her own as usual, wandered in. He bade the black and white Friesian good day, fed her some oats and barley, and put the machine to work to milk her. He then sat down in the empty stall next to her and proceeded to tell her all of his worries. She would occasionally raise her head from her food and look at him with those great eyes, seeming to say "whatever you say my friend, I totally agree". With an empty udder she inelegantly turned and plodded after her friends making their way to the grass field. Looking after the docile old lady he recalled last year when she had produced a premature calf under the hedge at the bottom of Stephens' field. When she failed to appear at the cowshed, he had gone to find her. There she was looking down proudly at her new creation. As Robert approached her she had lowered her head in a protective gesture threatening him. He had laughed and thrust his own heads gently into hers saying "You old fool, you know I'm not going to hurt your baby" and he had picked up the calf, no bigger than a small dog, and set off for the farm with Dolly plodding maternally along close behind him.

The machines all carefully washed, dairy floor swilled down and the churns put out on the stand ready for the milkman to collect them later that morning, he could now wash the cowshed floor down in case the hygiene lady came calling. "I wish she would smile sometimes" he thought "her face is mostly as long as our cows." Hungry now he made his way home, pedalling furiously and relishing the feel of the warm breeze in his face now that the rain had ceased, and feeling how good it was to exercise muscles which he hadn't used for some time.

Anne had prepared for him a full cooked breakfast of eggs, bacon and mushrooms saying that, now he was doing physical work, he would need the extra energy. "I don't want to see you fade away" she said with a smile. After breakfast Anne, Emily and Meg walked to the village to buy some food while Robert sat in the garden, mug of tea in hand, and plotted his next move. He was surprised to see a police car pull up in the lane outside his house, and wondered whether Pengelly had come to arrest him. However he was pleased to see the two London detectives Malcolm and Trevor alight from the car and come to join him in the garden. After the customary handshakes Trevor explained that they had heard of the latest murder, of Bill's arrest, and of Robert's suspension from duty. The two detectives had heard what had happened at the station from Arthur Vile, and were themselves unable to comprehend Pengelly's behaviour. The latter had ordered them to have nothing further to do with Robert, but they were happy to ignore that order, and, indeed said that they would be advising the superintendent of this when he arrived, suggesting that he should talk to Robert since he was the man who knew the area best. Trevor stated that, with the latest murder, and its proximity to the first one, both he and Malcolm felt more than ever that someone local, who knew the district was in all probability the perpetrator of the two crimes. Robert thought for a moment and replied "I certainly can't now rule out the possibility that someone from the local community is the culprit, or at least knows something about it though it grieves me to have to say that."

Bringing his two colleagues a cold drink he told them about his new job as a farm labourer, but said that despite his suspension he was determined to investigate the two crimes himself, and would welcome any intelligence they could give him. They wholeheartedly agreed to help him, pointing out that, now that Superintendent Weir was in charge, they could safely by-pass the irascible Inspector Pengelly. The two men then left to drive to the railway station to pick up their boss.

Anne returned from the village telling her husband how news of his suspension from the police had quickly spread through the tight-knit community. Robert surmised that it had been the Chalmers who had let the news out. He was totally unconcerned, and felt encouraged when Anne told him how everybody she had spoken to had offered their support to him and to his family. He could now outline his plan of action for the foreseeable future, until his suspension was cancelled. He told Anne that he would continue working for Dave, milking the cows twice a day and doing any other tasks the farmer had for him. He said that he was thoroughly enjoying being with the animals, and especially the riding of his bike once again. He said that he intended to examine more closely the two murder sites, and would rely on his old friend the prof to tell him the results of the post mortem of the latest casualty. He would also range widely over the many woods and fields between the two villagers and, to Anne's surprise stated that he was going to talk to his long-term adversary Ian Friend since he, together with old Bill, knew more about the countryside round about than anyone else. She concurred with this suggestion, but laughingly added that he must make sure that Ian didn't have a cricket ball with him.

Anne asked if she could help in any way but Robert, putting his arm round her, said "sweetheart, don't forget that two young women have been brutally murdered recently and I don't want you to put yourself in danger. I think you should stay close to home until we have apprehended this vicious brute. The two victims have both been young and pretty like you". "Why, thank you kind sir "she replied.

Cycling along the lane to the farm for his afternoon duties, his eye wandered to the brooding stand of great trees that constituted the forest where visitors were not welcomed. This stand of trees was called Oak Hill though there were more beech trees than oaks. Robert loved trees, and these, clothed in all their summer finery, looked particularly splendid. Even the conifers had a certain dark beauty contrasting with the many hues of green of the deciduous trees. Turning his gaze now to the right, he scanned the POW camp, and thought, despite Pengelly's commands, he would further explore that area, and talk to Dicky Smith again.

CHAPTER EIGHTEEN

Milking that afternoon was a joint effort with Dave helping, and while they worked the two chatted amiably about life in general. They discussed rationing and the state of the country, wondering what the world would look like in ten years' time. The USA was clearly now the top nation in the world, but strangely their former ally the Soviet Union, was increasingly regarded with suspicion. After talking about the cricket, the subject of the murders was raised by Robert. Milking over the two men followed the herd as they meandered to the grass meadow which abutted the wood where the first body had been found. Entering the trees to the annoyance of the many birds peacefully feeding there, they quartered the whole wood looking for anything out of the ordinary. They were aware that experts had already searched the area, but these men were strangers to the district, and were in all probability men from cities without the experience of rural life. Their exploration over, they then walked round the fences which enclosed the wood, looking for signs of entry, perhaps a fence post disturbed or the barbed wire with shreds of clothing. They found nothing out of the ordinary, and returned to the farm where Robert bade his friend farewell and mounted his bike for the ride home. As he pedalled unhurriedly along the lane he was reminded of a poem which he had recited to the parents at an open day at the school. "I love the little winding lanes, In the sweet days when summer reigns…" Memories of his school days were always happy ones for him as it was there that he had first met Anne. When he got home he would remind her of that!

He was surprised to see that he had a visitor. Sitting in the garden, talking to Anne and Emily was Ian Friend. The poacher and fast bowler stood up to greet Robert saying "I hear they've sacked you, so I can carry on catching my rabbits, pheasants, hares and partridges without having to keep out of your way, not that you were ever good enough to catch me!" this said with a broad smile. "Seriously, you're not bad for a copper, even if, for a batsman, you're an easy wicket for a quick bowler." The two men grinned and Anne was relieved to see that there was no animosity between the two large men. They sat now and Anne went to fetch cold drinks for them. Robert thought for a while and then said "I'm going to try and solve these two murders and get old Bill out of that awful prison cell. I've already had a close look at the wood where the first attack took place. I went there with Dave Chalmers, and I now want to have a look at the spot where the other murder took place once the detectives have finished their investigation. I reckon you know more about the area than anybody else. How about coming with me when I'm prowling about? I want to have a look at all of the copses and woods between the two villages, and I want to probe the ground around the POW camp. I can't go in as Taffy Pengelly might be a bit upset, but he can't stop me from walking round the perimeter."

The two men were chatting almost like old friends. They actually had two things in common- they were both keen, and indeed talented cricketers, each with their own speciality. Then there was the practising poacher and the erstwhile one- both ideally suited to the exploration of their territory. When Robert brought up the subject of Oak Hill the forbidding forest, Ian looked doubtful. He explained that, when the wood belonged to Dave Chalmers both he and old Bill had roamed freely in there in search of prey. However, since it had been fenced off, he had steered clear of the place, and said that he himself had heard odd sounds emanating from the trees sometimes in the evening or at night. He said that there had always been evidence of badgers there with enormous setts. When Robert told of his intention of entering the forest Ian looked doubtful, but then smilingly stated "Well I'd better come with you or you could find yourself lost." Ian said that he had always wondered how the wood had got its name, but he went on to say that all of the woods, fields and lanes had some sort of name, the derivation of which was lost in the mists of history. For example he said that one of Jim Bailey's fields was called Little Meadows, yet it was far and away the biggest on his farm. Robert shook Ian's hand as he rose to leave, and he realised that a friendship which had until now seemed highly un likely, had been established, and he was happy at the thought.

The following morning when he returned from the farm, Anne told him that Trevor, one of the detectives, had called round to tell him that his Superintendent would like to talk to him, together with the prof. He said that they would be at the King's Arms at lunchtime today, and asked Robert to meet them there. With a smile Anne said "You men will always find an excuse to go to the pub." Then she kissed her husband and he set off on his bike to the village and his local watering hole.

The landlord, Stan, pointed to the snug bar from where voices could be heard. As he entered he saw Trevor and Malcolm seated at a table together with a very large man, all three nursing mugs of ale. Offering a large, meaty hand, Superintendent Weir boomed you must be that naughty constable who has grievously offended your Inspector Pengelly. Shaking his hand Robert noted the broad Scottish accent and responded by saying "we don't often get famous coppers here in our neck of the woods sir. Forgive me if I'm a bit overwhelmed". Chuckling the officer replied "Don't get too used to it laddie. All these trees, fields, huge smelly animals and twittering birds are not my cup of tea. I've migrated from the far north, and I prefer noisy, crowded streets and leery villains. Mind you there's one of these baddies come amongst you at the moment I'm told, and I'm here to help you sort him, them or her out. Meantime I'll try and ignore the fact that you're a disgraced cop, but I'm in desperate need of someone who knows the area and the local villains."

Robert took to this large, bluff policeman. This was a no nonsense official who would surely get things done. Everything about the man was massive. A great round, red face sporting a handlebar moustache, brown with flecks of grey in it, an equally round head, totally hairless, and as red as his face. He sat there looking like a Buddha, in a grey three-piece suit, the waistcoat bulging over a gargantuan belly. This was one impressive human being. As Robert studied the superintendent, the snug door opened and the ever untidy prof shambled in, greeting all, and parking his substantial posterior on a chair. "Sorry I'm late" he chirped, beaming round the table. Looking at the glasses on the table he boomed "This is a dry old job isn't it?" Robert called out to the landlord who soon appeared with a foaming tankard of beer for the parched scientist.

"What we are doing here is, for the moment, unofficial, because, as we are all aware Bob Evans is suspended, at least until I can override the suspension" began the superintendent. "I have spoken to Pengelly, but he is refusing to reverse his decision and at the moment I am unable to override his ruling. However put that aside for the moment. I am not interested in office feuds. We have two murders to solve, certainly with some local involvement, and we need a local man to assist us. So Mister Evans you are a part of this team, reporting only to me. Is that OK?" Robert nodded his agreement. The prof then chipped in, wiping the froth of his beer from his lips with a beefy hand. "I have examined the latest murder victim and can, without hesitation, state that both are connected. The only difference is that some attempt had been made to cover the second girl's body. They are both young girls in their twenties and previously in good health. They are Caucasian, neatly, but not extravagantly dressed. The contents of their stomachs were quite similar with evidence of largely vegetables having been ingested. This I would have expected anyway because of the rationing. The first victim had a perfect set of teeth, but this one had had two fillings, and we can see that the dentistry is not British in nature, rather continental, and perhaps to the East of Europe. The fatal injuries were both inflicted by a similar cutting instrument, and in neither case is there signs of a struggle. Gentlemen here endeth the report of the medical practitioners, I now leave it to you, the elite of the gendarmerie, to discover the identity of the murderous knaves who have interrupted the gentle tenor of my life." Raising his empty tankard high in the air, he bellowed "Proprietor, has the tide gone out? I appear to be need of yet more of your splendid tipple".

All glasses now refilled, the super then began meticulously to review the situation, asking questions of the others as he himself became better acquainted with the facts of the two cases. He said that he had told Pengelly that he was now in complete charge of the investigation, but had not told him that he was going to involve Constable Evans. Incidentally he said that when he had said to the inspector "yakki Da"- the only Welsh he knew- the latter had simply looked at him as though he was gone out. Malcolm stated that the inspector had become more and more erratic since the two murders, and was prone to outbursts of temper, often muttering under his breath in a language they assumed to be Welsh.

"Of course" interjected the prof, "the strangest thing of all is the scar on the back of victim number two, almost exactly mirroring that on the skin of the first poor young lady. The scar is of the same length, and again seems to have been an attempt to erase some sort of tattoo. Possibly four letters or characters have been crudely effaced, but in each case the concealment has not been totally successful. As we know, with the first scar, the first letter a "c" was still discernible, and with the latest victim the last letter, possibly "p" is just visible. Thus gentlemen, you must now fathom out what the missing symbols are, and that, I hasten to add, will go a long way to solving the mystery". With that the prof sat back, his attention now completely focussed on the contents of his tankard.

The superintendent thanked Doctor Buchanan and then asked the scientist "What about time of death, Doctor?" Reluctantly he put down his glass, belched softly and affirmed that both killings had been carried out during the hours of darkness, probably in the early hours. "As he spoke his eye was drawn to the large pike in the glass case on the wall "who caught that great beast?" he exclaimed. At which Robert admitted that no-one knew who had caught the fish, and indeed where it had been netted, but it certainly was not in the little stream which ran through the village. Some previous landlord had displayed the unlikely monster purely to provoke interest and speculation. "Just another fishy tale then", chortled the prof.

While they all tucked into a ploughman's of delicious home-made bread and, despite the rationing, a generous portion of cheese, the super laid out the tactics for the coming days. He said that the patrols would resume to reassure the villagers. With Stan's co-operation a command centre would be set up in the large committee room at the rear of the pub. At that the prof's eyes lit up and he confirmed that he would be a frequent visitor, for professional purposes only of course. The landlord rubbed his hands at the thought of the extra business, it was like Christmas had come early. When Robert told Superintendent Weir that there was much disquiet in the two villages, the latter resolved to have uniformed officers on foot patrol until such time as the culprit or culprits had been apprehended. He added that it might be wise if the ladies, particularly the young ones, remained at home during the hours of darkness. While every little detail of the murders was being reported to the brains of London, and indeed of Europe, the search would now concentrate locally.

Having been informed of the problems Robert had encountered at the POW camp, the super said that he himself would pay it a visit, having first spoken to the military authorities beforehand. Then, tapping Robert on the arm he told him that he would urgently seek the release of Bill, and have him taken home on bail. He thanked the officer, and asked if he minded if he, together with Ian, did some probing in the more remote areas of the countryside. "An interesting pair of sleuths "said Weir, "a suspended copper and a known law-breaker. Like Sherlock Holmes and Watson!" He told Robert to go ahead, and to report daily to him at the pub. Then he roared "and don't think that rogue Friend will get paid for his efforts!" The meeting over, they all dispersed and went their various ways, the prof looking back sorrowfully at the pub sign. Getting into his car the superintendent said to Robert "They tell me you are now a farm labourer. Well my granddad farmed in Perthshire, and I used to enjoy going to his farm to help out with the animals. When I get a bit of spare time I'll put my wellies on and join you in the cowshed." "You'd be very welcome sir" re-joined Robert, "but remember, suspended or not, on the farm I'm in charge"

CHAPTER NINETEEN

For the next few days the momentarily at least, ex-policeman Robert Evans, together with his reprobate friend Ian roamed the countryside looking for something which could lead them to a significant clue which might solve the enigma of the murders. He was content to let Ian lead the way, bowing to his greater understanding of the area. With his work on Dave's farm and his daily walks through the woods and fields, he felt strangely satisfied with his present life. As ordered he reported each day to the super at the pub, being careful not to yield to the temptation of sampling a pint of beer at every visit. Not surprisingly the prof always seemed to be there, liquid refreshment in hand, now a firm pal of Stan the proprietor. Despite the exhaustive enquiries into the two murders being made no meaningful progress had been made. The tattoo on the girls' backs was baffling everyone. Code breakers and crossword aficionados were given the task of unravelling the mystery, but, thus far, to no avail. At the station a blackboard had been set up, and the local bobbies were invited to write their own thoughts on four letter words beginning "c" and ending "p". The majority of the submissions were obviously done tongue in cheek, and some simply proved that lessons in spelling were required. Unsurprisingly the word CRAP was the most popular suggestion, but was ruled out by an increasingly frustrated Sergeant Vile who had installed the blackboard. Something which he now regretted. The blackboard was soon dispatched to the storeroom at the back of the station. The atmosphere in the cop shop was decidedly frosty with everyone at some time being harshly criticised by an increasingly bad-tempered Inspector Pengelly.

Came the long awaited day when old Bill was released from his lonely prison cell, and brought home in a police car. Sister Liz together with Robert and Anne, and most of the village people were eagerly awaiting his arrival. As he entered his garden Liz presented him with his shining, new looking bicycle, and she hugged her brother seeing how emotional he was. Waving his thanks, he mounted his faithful old steed and raced away down the lane, the applause of his neighbours ringing in his ears.

Robert and Ian were systematically quartering the area of woods, thickets and fields along the valley between the two hamlets. They talked a lot as they walked and, despite their different backgrounds, were fast becoming friends. Ian told his partner that he was looking at the natural world in a different way from what he was used to. He said that usually he was seeking the tell-tale signs of rabbits, badgers and other mammals which frequented the woods. Now he was searching the ground for unusual indications of human activity. Laughingly he joked to Robert that they were like Sherlock Holmes and Watson seeking out Moriarty. His companion replied that, in that case he ought to smoke a large pipe and wear a deerstalker hat. Despite the good humour they were both carefully intent on finding anything which did not fit into the landscape. On their way they met and talked to farmers and their workers always asking the question "Have you seen anything abnormal hereabouts recently?" After some days of tiring walking up hills and along steep banks and through thick hedges they had found nothing suspicious, and rather disappointingly the team at the pub had nothing of import to share with them either.

The two sleuths decided therefore to take a day off. Apart from the daily chore of milking, Dave had a number of jobs he would like Robert to do on the farm. When he asked the farmer if Ian too could help, he slowly shook his head saying that he didn't completely trust the young fast bowler/poacher. He said that he had had issues with the Friend family in the past. Robert could understand Chalmers' doubts about Ian, and, as a policeman he had himself had run ins with Ian's father and his uncle, both of whom had spent time inside a prison at his majesty's pleasure. However he pointed out that they were not violent by nature, and their crimes had been all quite minor, and indeed both the older Friends had fought in the recent war, and had conducted themselves with dignity. Robert understood Dave's' reluctance to employ the Friend lad, and did not push the point any further. When told about the superintendent's farming background Dave said that the officer was welcome to visit his farm whenever he wanted to.

So intent was Robert on his farming and sleuthing that he realised that he was neglecting his family, so he made a point of going home whenever he could to see Anne and to play with Emily and Meg. The weather that summer continued to be benevolent with only the occasional rain shower and none of the customary noisy thunderstorms. Day by day the sun shone, the skies were a bright blue and a breeze wafted the smells of the countryside across the landscape. Fluffy happy white clouds chased each other across the boundless heavens. Despite his present work predicament, he was grateful at not having to wear his heavy police uniform. He had always been popular with the villagers and found that, now that he was just one of them, they greeted him with greater warmth than before. He had a good working relationship with the policemen who he met regularly at the pub.

Old Bill, sitting proudly atop his radiant newly re-furbished bicycle, waved ever more enthusiastically as he raced by Robert's cottage, and rabbits continued to mysteriously appear on the doorstep. He could not understand how the old man managed to catch the furry little creatures since he and Ian, in their hunts through the territory, had never caught sight of the wily old man.

Beginning the milking one afternoon Robert, and Dave Chalmers were surprised and delighted to see Superintendent Weir enter the cowshed, sporting a pair of immaculate black wellington boots. Introduced to Dave, he asked if he could help. Without demur the farmer provided him with a rather scruffy overall, and stood back to see if the large policeman knew what he was doing. He need not have been concerned as he watched him attach the cups to Dora's teats, and stand back to watch the milk flow. "I think we can leave him to it " said Robert, but they stayed to work together until all of the cows were relieved of their milk, and let loose to return to their pasture. Then the three men adjourned to the farmhouse where Julie brewed tea and presented her own scones, with home-made butter and raspberry jam. Overflowing an overstuffed armchair the genial superintendent expressed his appreciation for the refreshments, and stated that he was considering moving his headquarters from the pub to this welcoming farmhouse venue. Robert thought that that was a first class idea, but he felt that the prof might miss the ale provided by the King's Arms.

Time to leave, the three men walked to the super's car, where they stood for a while basking in the grandeur of the countryside. Pensively Reg Weir breathed "You are very lucky to live here in this beautiful place. It makes me even more determined to sort out this mess and to restore your world to the way it was always intended to be". Turning to Robert, he pointed to the whole vista in front of him and asked him "Have you, and your scouting friend been through all of this"? He illustrated this with a sweep of a meaty arm, and looked enquiringly at him. "All except the POW camp directly in front of you, and Pengelly has ordered me not to go there, and the forest behind the camp. That used to belong to Dave but was bought some time ago by some mysterious company. Since then it has been fenced off, and trespassers are not welcomed." Weir pondered for a moment then, thoughtfully stroking his chin, said to Robert. "Leave the camp to me. I'll invite your pal Dicky Smith for a drink at the pub. You must join us too and we'll ask a few more questions about the prison. From here, with the big fences, the barbed wire and the one entrance, it looks pretty secure, but we'll wait until we've spoken to the corporal. As for the forest I'll have to rely on you and Mister Friend to explore there. I'm essentially a city man nowadays, and wouldn't really know what I was looking for. I'll try to make discreet enquiries to find out who are the mysterious owners of that piece of woodland." With that the burly policeman shook hands warmly with the farmer, and said that he would love to help out with the milking again sometime. Dave replied that he would be more than welcome any time, and he stood at the farm gate as the two policemen left.

Cycling home, his thoughts everywhere but on the tarmac in front of him, Robert was awoken from his reverie by the noise of bicycle tyres rapidly coming up behind him. Turning his head he saw a beaming Bill, one hand on the handlebars of his rejuvenated machine, the other brandishing a plump rabbit which he promptly presented to his friend. Robert thanked the old poacher who responded with a broad smile. They then rode together in companiable silence with Bill pointing now and again at things which pleased him, like small songbirds flitting about in the hedgerows beside the lane. He would then cup his ear with one hand rejoicing in the melodious sound of his feathered pals. His obvious delight was echoed by Robert, and they rode side by side along the winding, narrow lane trusting to luck that there was no other traffic on that road. A loud blast on a car horn caused both men to swerve violently to the side of the lane, on to the grass verge, and they stopped to allow a police car to pass. Glaring from the back seat of the vehicle was none other than Inspector Pengelly. Robert completely ignored his tormentor, but Bill gave his erstwhile gaoler a boisterous two fingered salute as the car accelerated away. The two men, smiles returning to their faces, now went on their way. Passing the Brisley smallholding Robert was relieved to see that two venerable ladies were nowhere to be seen, and he wouldn't have to politely refuse the offer of yet another Guinness!

CHAPTER TWENTY

The council of war was convened once again in the comfortable surroundings of the pub. Conducting proceedings was Superintendent Weir, and also present were Robert Evans, Corporal Dicky Smith, and the additional invitee Ian Friend. The latter because of his knowledge of the land surrounding the POW camp. Doctor Buchanan, the prof, had also felt it necessary to attend, the lure of foaming pints of bitter of course having nothing to do with his presence. The landlord having been ordered to keep the door of the room firmly closed, the meeting could now commence.

Weir began to interrogate, politely but firmly, the army corporal. Robert was highly impressed at the policeman's incisive manner, and could instantly see how the bluff Scotsman had been assigned to this baffling case. He wanted to know the history of the camp, where the inmates had come from, how and when they had arrived there, and the precise security arrangements that obtained there. Dicky explained that the camp had apparently been established during the First World War, initially for German soldiers, and some sailors. When these men had been repatriated, the site was left abandoned until it was re-instated when the more recent conflict had flared up. He said that although he was not there when it was opened up again in 1943. He had heard that chaos had reigned for a while when the new batch of Italian servicemen had arrived on the scene. There had been too few guards, and the management was totally inadequate. There was accommodation, basically Nissan huts, for one thousand men, but nearly double that number had de-bussed at the gate on that first day. He said that, when he had been posted there, some months after it had opened, he had found that the record keeping was inadequate and he didn't believe that an accurate figure had ever been produced of the number of prisoners. The guards then, and now were generally older men looking forwards to retirement with no incentive to be efficient. The officer who had taken charge when the camp opened was himself a World War One veteran within a few short months of his own demob.

The superintendent asked the soldier to go through the daily routine at the prison, and DIcky took him through the guarding procedure, the daily release of those working locally, and the twice daily roll call. There were, at present, some five hundred detainees with a number being repatriated each month. He said that the site would become empty in less than a year. Of course, as there were fewer POWs now, some of the guards had been posted away, and the older ones demobbed. Pausing to take a drink Corporal Smith frankly admitted that the running of the camp was hardly a shining example of efficiency. He himself would be glad to leave, and he felt that the villagers too, although not at all worried about the prisoners themselves, would be relieved to see this reminder of a savage war vacant once more, or better still demolished.

Ian had been sitting listening intently to the corporal, and he held his hand up wanting to say something. Seeing this Robert was reminded of the school classroom with a pupil eagerly wanting to answer a question, or perhaps seeking permission to go to the toilet. "I've not been in the camp obviously" said the ex-poacher, "but I have hunted round the perimeter looking for rabbits, and I've never seen anything unusual inside the camp. Apart from the wooded area at the rear of the installation, the land is fairly flat and open, mostly rough grassland with a few stunted bushes. Looking in to the camp you can see the prisoners walking together, chatting, smoking or kicking an old football about. There doesn't seem to be any sign of tension in there, and the guards mingle happily with their charges. The security fences seem to be in good order, and, as far as I can see, they have not been tampered with in any way."

The superintendent thanked Ian for his comments, but grinned when the precocious young man suggested that he be put on the police payroll. "But I don't want one of those pointy helmets, sir, my head's the wrong shape!" At this hilarity the super thought that they had done as much as they could for today. He thanked everybody for their attention, and said that he would be paying a visit to the POW camp as soon as he had informed the authorities of his intention. He said that, since there had been two murders and he needed to eliminate the occupants of the prison from his inquiry, he felt that it would be unreasonable of the army to deny him access. When Robert warned him to take care with the hut where he had been assaulted, he replied with a knowing smile "Don't you worry, I'll have the heavy mob with me."" What about Pengelly?" asked the prof to which the reply was "You leave him to me, I don't think he'll suspend me!"

As they all rose to leave, with the prof gazing wistfully at his now empty beer glass, Robert told the super that he and Ian intended to probe the forest the next day, and asked what the legal position would be if they were caught. "It's only ten years for trespass" said Weir, clapping Ian heartily on the back. "But I'll get your sentences reduced for good behaviour". The two civilian sleuths smiled, and felt completely confident that the superintendent would indeed back them up whatever happened.

As he milked the cows that afternoon, Robert was mulling over how best to tackle the search through the forest. Where best to enter the trees, and at what time of the day would suit Ian, knowing that the lad would have to carry on doing some work to earn money. Chores of the day completed, he stood with Dave Chalmers, leaning on the field gate looking over the fields towards the trees, glowing golden in the rays of the late afternoon sun. As the farmer contentedly puffed away on his old pipe, Robert asked him if he regretted selling the wood. "Not really" he answered, "it's very beautiful, and I love trees, but financially it wasn't worth holding on to, and when I received a surprisingly generous offer for it, I couldn't refuse. We spent the money on doing up some of the old farm buildings, bought a new tractor and", grinning at his companion, "bought the wife a couple of new dresses. When it belonged to us, we would often walk through the trees to listen to the birds, and to enjoy the tranquillity of the place. Occasionally I would take my twelve bore up there to shoot a pigeon, or a pheasant, during the season of course. I never stopped anyone from enjoying the wood and I know that many people liked to stroll through the trees on fine days, taking in the tranquillity of the place."

There was a silence between the two of them as they took in the peaceful scene, the quiet disturbed only by the steady munching of the dairy herd a few yards away from them as they rhythmically chewed their way through the nourishing grass. "One slightly odd thing happened early in the war" said Dave. "It was 1940 in the autumn when I received a visit from an army officer, don't know what rank he was but he was clearly someone of importance. He told me that the army was to take over the forest for some time and that, until he came to tell me that they had finished their work, nobody was to enter the trees. He did not explain the purpose of their work, and I just assumed it was something to do with the war. They were only there for a month or so. I did as I was told and stayed out of the wood, but I did, from time to time, walk along the edge, being nosy I suppose. There was a lot of activity in there with some vehicle noise. Then, one day, the same officer came to the farm and said that they had finished and that we could go into the wood whenever we wanted. He thanked me, gave my wife a nice bunch of flowers, and gave me a voucher for fuel for the tractor which was very welcome". Once the soldiers had left I did go into the trees to get some idea what they had been doing, but, apart from tyre marks and evidence of many feet having trampled around, I could not see anything out of the ordinary. Certainly the birds were still chattering away in the undergrowth and the treetops, and at night we could still see the bats flying about. The old fox continued to give voice during the hours of darkness, and the little owl answered angrily."

Robert listened with interest to what Dave had to say and replied "Lots of things happened during the war years, and maybe, sometime in the future, many secrets will be revealed." "Ay" replied the farmer "and maybe we might wish that some of those secrets remain secret."

On his way home he mulled over what Dave had told him of the wartime activities in the increasingly mysterious forest, but felt that events that had happened years ago now, strange though they might have seemed at the time, probably bore no relevance to the present situation. Nonetheless he would bear it in mind when he and Ian began their recce of the wood. Perhaps he could ask Superintendent Weir to seek the help of the War Office to further unravel the mysteries of Oak Hill.

CHAPTER TWENTY-ONE

The two intrepid explorers, the disgraced copper and his poacher sidekick duly climbed the high fence surrounding the trees, carefully avoiding the barbed wire atop the fence, and, once inside, walking some twenty yards apart, began to look for anything which jarred with the wooded environment. It was evening and cool under the canopy of the towering beech, ash and oak trees. Brambles, nettles and squat shrubs were everywhere, and the many rabbit holes threatened sprained ankles to the unwary visitor. Ian called Robert over at one point to show him a spectacularly large badger sett with marks all round of the animals' paw prints. However, as they progressed through the slowly darkening wood they saw no animals, only myriads of butterflies, moths and other insects, and there was very little birdsong. Probably the feathered creatures had been frightened away by the two clumsy humans invading their territory.

The two scouts spent nearly three hours going over every inch of the forest, and eventually emerged at the same point at which they had entered. There was evidence of human activity, footprints, and one discarded cigarette end, but they felt that this was probably from men employed by the owners to keep an eye on their property. Robert suggested to Ian that, on their way home they might just walk round the perimeter of the POW camp. Ian reluctantly agreed saying that he had already done that many times, and had found nothing of interest, and pointed out that he was now a little thirsty and the Kings Arms wasn't far away! Thus it was a rapid stroll round the prison, keeping their eyes open, and waving to the prisoners who crowded to the wire to greet them. As ever they made no attempt to penetrate the tangle of thorn bushes and brambles at the far end of the compound, and they decided to end their day's sleuthing and go their own ways, Robert to his home and Ian to the pub. Robert was disappointed that he had nothing of substance to report to the superintendent.

When the "War party" next met at their watering hole the King's Arms, Superintendent Weir announced that the local press had now been given details of the strange mutilations on the two girls' backs. The hope was that some member of the reading public could throw some light on the matter. He further announced that he had told Inspector Pengelly that Robert was helping him with the enquiries. Looking at him he said "I can't yet overrule your suspension Evans, but I will give evidence on your behalf when the disciplinary body meets to decide your fate". Robert thanked him, and Ian jokingly asked if all of his poaching offences could now be stricken from the records too. The bluff Scotsman retorted that it rather depended on how well he behaved in the next few days or weeks.

Some days later, on a blustery, rain soaked evening, as Robert and Anne settled down to listening to a concert of Johann Strauss on the radio, there was a timid knock on their front door. Meg of course ran to see who it was, giving her little warning yelps, and Anne quickly hushed her, not wanting to have Emily woken. Robert opened the door to see his old Head master Patrick Burr standing there, looking very bedraggled, quite unlike his usual immaculate self. Inviting the old teacher in Robert shook his hand and led him into the living room where Anne greeted him, asked him to sit and went to make a cup of tea for the wet old pedagogue. Satisfied that the newcomer offered no threat, Meg retreated to her bed and promptly fell asleep.

Mr. Burr, now comfortingly settled in to his arm chair, wiped the rain from his spectacles, and smiled benignly at his old pupils. Tea and cakes produced, vision restored, Robert gently asked the reason for his visit. "It's really grand to see you sir, but what possessed you to venture out on such an awful evening?" From his raincoat pocket Mr Burr produce a copy of the Times newspaper, and, on the front page, pointed to an article about the two murders in the village and the scars which, thus far, had baffled the brains of the police forces. Robert concurred that they had not yet found the significance of the "c" followed by possibly two spaces and the "p". Everybody felt that, unravelling this mystery, was probably the key to solving the two hideous crimes. Mr Burr was a linguist who, before taking up the post of Headmaster at the local school, had taught a number of European languages at the Grammar School, and had turned down the post of interpreter at the Nuremberg Trials. He now pointed out to Robert that there were other alphabets than the one used by English speakers. "My thinking is that maybe we should be looking at the Cyrillic Alphabet". Both Anne and Robert looked bemused, since, apart from some Italian which Robert had picked up during his war service, neither had studied languages at school.

The former teacher stood up, and, going to the dining table, asked for pencil and paper. He when wrote c……p, and next to it s……r. Seeing the lack of understanding on the faces of his two ex-pupils, he explained that, in the Cyrillic Alphabet c is actually an s, and p an r." Now" he went on," perhaps if we make an educated guess and fill in the missing two letters with s, we arrive at SSSR. This we should better recognise as USSR, or," Anne interjected, "The Soviet Union!" Nodding happily to her Mr Burr said "Correct, the Union Of Soviet Socialist Republics."

Robert studied the writing for some time then said, "Well, it's the first explanation of any sort we have had thus far, but, if your thinking is correct, it actually deepens the mystery of the two deaths. It certainly adds a new and strangely different dimension to the affair. I will certainly bear it in mind and mention it when I next meet the detectives. I must thank you for trying to help us in our endeavours." Talk then turned to matters educational as school days were re-lived, and the two ex-pupils were enthralled as the Head described in some detail of life in the school during the war years, of having no electricity, no running water, outside toilets, gas masks, lessons in the air-raid shelter, constant air activity while the Battle of Britain raged in the skies above, and, towards the latter end of the conflict, the dreaded doodlebugs. Then, as the conversation began to falter, Mr Burr rose to leave, thanking Anne for her hospitality. At the door Robert, in his turn, thanked the elderly teacher for his interest, and watched him set off along the lane towards his own little cottage. The rain had now stopped and it was a perfect summer night, with a bright full moon, and a myriad of stars twinkling in the firmament.

A blustery, but warm wind tousled his blonde locks as Robert walked briskly down to the village to meet with the Superintendent and his minions in the pub. His eye was caught by a flock of pigeons frantically flying to the safety of the trees, behind them a streamlined Harris Hawk, straining every sinew to snatch his breakfast. Admiring the variegated greenery of the forest, and thinking of the teacher's visit of the evening before, he was minded of a poem written by one of the other teachers at the school.

Mary Godden had written of her own favourite wood:

> "O come ye with me to the home of my childhood
> To the old-fashioned farmstead that nestles below,
> I'll show you the beauties of all the green wildwood.
> To the haunts of the bluebell and cowslip we'll go."

As he entered the "war room" Robert was surprised, and not a little concerned to see Inspector Pengelly seated at the table. He glowered at Robert who stared wooden-faced at his tormentor. Superintendent Weir, noting the antipathy between the pair, stated "Although he is temporarily, and I stress temporarily, suspended from duty, I have brought him in on this enquiry for his local knowledge. I regard him as an important member of the team." Pengelly's sour face told its own story, but he knew that he had to accept his superior's authority. However, when Ian Friend strolled casually into cheerfully greet everyone, the inspector, eyes bulging and crimson of face blurted out "surely we're not using criminals too on this case. This man has a criminal record as long as my arm." "And I love you too inspector" retorted Ian. Calmly Weir explained that the poacher was helping Robert on scouring the area looking for clues. The inspector seemed to shrink visibly in his seat, as Weir asked "has anyone got anything new for us today?"

Robert hesitated before reporting what his old Headmaster had suggested might be the meaning of the awful bodged scarring on the backs of the two girls. Pengelly's reaction was one of utter disbelief. He muttered incoherently under his breath before blurting out "This is absolute nonsense, suggesting some flimsy connection with the Soviet Union or another country of Eastern Europe. This is, after the United Kingdom, and here we use our own alphabet. We should continue to assume that the recognisable letters are "c" and "p" and forget this foreign nonsense, invented by a doddery old teacher." Robert bridled at that and told the inspector that Mr Burr was a respected academic and not given to flights of fancy. Intervening before the animosity between the two men spilled over into something physical. The Superintendent said with authority "the teacher's observation may well be fanciful but, at the moment we have nothing else to go on, so I shall inform the security services of this, and leave it to them to investigate further. In the meantime let's all keep our ears and eyes open to see if we can achieve a breakthrough". Snorting angrily, Pengelly got up abruptly, spilling his chair as he did so, and marched from the room, again muttering under his breath. As he left Ian called out "Bye, it was a pleasure to see you inspector!"

CHAPTER TWENTY-TWO

As the days passed into weeks, and August put in an appearance. Now a different routine became the norm. Meetings in the Kings Arms were not so frequent now, much to the disappointment of the ale-loving prof. Superintendent Weir spent much of his time now in consultation with the spooks of the security service in London. None of these worthies had felt the need to visit the scenes of the crimes, relying instead on the information gleaned by the locals like Robert and Ian. Old Bill was an ever-present in the lanes and around the villages, astride his gleaming bike, handlebars usually festooned with rabbits he had killed. Anne was rapidly running out of new recipes for the furry creatures. Robert continued to work on Dave Chalmers' farm, and thoroughly enjoyed being with the animals. Anne and Emily joined him most days, and his little daughter was beginning to look and sound like a farmer herself. She showed no fear of the large dairy cows, and the farm dogs followed her wherever she went. Dave's wife was very impressed how the dogs would obey the little girl's every command, from" sit" ,"stay", "heel". The animals had never been so obedient.

Superintendent Weir took every opportunity on his visits to the village to join Robert and Dave Chalmers in milking the cows. He was rapidly getting to know many of the locals who were becoming used to his, to them, unfamiliar accents. The Brisley sisters in particular took to the big man, who fortunately had a taste for Guinness, Robert made excuses not to accompany him when he went to see the redoubtable ladies, quite happy to see him devour the rich, dark ale. The super made a point of telling Doctor Buchanan of each and every visit he had made to see the two old ladies, tormenting the prof with his colourful descriptions of delicious luncheons in their kitchen, and endless bottles of the Irish liquid nectar.

The cricket season was now at its peak with two games each weekend, and occasionally a mid-week match as well. Robert's team was having a good season with most of the results going their way. Robert himself had become what the skipper called him "a run machine", rarely failing to notch up a big score. Even the three deckchair aficionados thought that he was not a bad batsman, but not yet as good as some of the old bats. Ian too was taking plenty of wickets for Hawksmead, without bowling any more bouncers. Both he and Robert were keenly anticipating the return match between the two villagers towards the end of the season.

After an infuriating delay, the CO of the POW camp at last granted permission for Superintendent Weir to enter the facility, strictly under army supervision. The police officer duly arrived, accompanied by two constables, and, at his own request, Inspector Pengelly. Weir was surprised to see that the inspector had a side-arm attached to his belt. When asked about this Pengelly replied that there were many prisoners here, until recently enemies of ours, and some might still want to avenge comrades who had died during the war. Weir shrugged his shoulders and made no further comment. He felt that it was an odd thing to do since the guards would be there to protect them in the unlikely event that they received a hostile reception.

At the gate the police were met by Corporal Smith and an officer bearing the insignia of a captain. Both of the military men bore arms. The captain, clearly not at ease, did not offer a name but led the police on a tour of the camp. He said very little, and left it to the corporal to tell the visitors all about the prison. Corporal Smith said that there were now only 300 hundred Italian soldiers remaining there, as, each month, more and more were repatriated. He stated that, in just a few months the facility would be empty, all of the prisoners back home, and the guards, like him, re-assigned to other duties, or, in some cases, demobbed. When Weir asked how it was decided which of the detainees would be the next to go, Smith, realising that his officer was showing no interest, explained that each man was interviewed to see who should be allowed to leave first. For example, he said that there were some soldiers who had been wounded, and were still in need of some further medical treatment. Married men too were given priority over the single men. When asked about any men who had caused disciplinary problems while in the camp, Dicky said that there had been very few problems as the men simply wanted to go home as soon as possible, and were not going to break the rules to prevent this. The corporal added that, in fact another twenty soldiers were to be shipped out today.

The inspection party walked all-round the camp, and were greeted amicably by most of the inmates. They went into the huts to see the facilities there, and also examined some of the now vacant billets, which were now bare rooms, everything having been taken away. They inspected the toilet blocks, the little hospital, and the larger huts where the meals were served. They were offered refreshments but the captain brusquely intervened by saying that there was no time for that, and they reluctantly moved on. The superintendent ordered the two constables, without asking the permission of the unhelpful military officer, to carefully examine the high fences which surrounded the camp to look for any evidence that they had been tampered with in any way. They reported that everything seemed to be in order. As they progressed from building to building, Inspector Pengelly offered to go himself to the hut at the top of the compound where Robert had had the run-in with the aggressive prisoner and check on it himself. Weir told him to go ahead since he was thinking that their visit had largely been a waste of time, and he could see no possible connection to the deaths of the girls. The inspector returned after a few minutes to report that everything seemed to be in order.

Back at the gate, while they waited for the inspector, the rather disgruntled captain wished them good-day and with a sloppy salute got into his car and drove off without a backward glance. Seeing the embarrassment on the corporal's face Reg Weir said "Don't worry Dicky, I met some Ruperts like that in my days in khaki." Back in the patrol car the superintendent said to his two companions "The Kings Arms if you please, I'll stand you two a pint, and we'll forget we're on duty." Smiling, the driver replied "thank you sir, we can't refuse an offer like that." He then added "Do you think the prof will be there sir?"

The sound of a horn meant that they had to wait as a large army lorry emerged from the prison and slowly passed them in the direction of the village. From the back of the vehicle men stood waving and shouting "Bye Bye England". They were a bunch of clearly happy people, excited at the thought of seeing their homeland and their families again soon. Dicky said that they would be shouting and waving all the long journey to the harbour where a ship would be waiting to give them the cruise of their lives.

The Superintendent reported on the apparently fruitless visit to the camp, and, almost at a loss concerning the investigation, asked the assembled fellow detectives for ideas. Pengelly felt that they had exhausted all possible leads, and that they should scale down the search for the culprits. They all looked at the inspector in amazement, and it was Robert who angrily retorted "No way, my community has been violated, two young women have been slaughtered and the people expect us to find the truth. They will not feel safe until the perpetrators have been caught. Reg Weir concurred and firmly assured them that he would not give up until the killer or killers had been found and brought to justice. He then asked Robert and Ian if there was any part, however small, of the area that they had not yet explored. Looking at Robert Ian replied that they had been very careful and exhaustive in their searching. Robert agreed with his fellow bloodhound, and went on to suggest that they might possibly now go over the same ground in the hours of darkness. Nodding Ian added "why don't we take your little dog with us to see if her sensitive nose might discover something we've missed?" Seeing the wisdom of this suggestion, Robert agreed, but laughingly pointed out that he would have to ask Emily's permission first.

Robert and Ian then went to the Evans' cottage where they were welcomed by Anne, Emily and Meg. They were a little surprised to find Liz sitting in the kitchen enjoying a cup of tea. On seeing the two men arrive she rose to leave but Robert asked her to stay. She had simply come to have a friendly chat to Anne, having few real friends of her own. The men explained that they were going to search through the woods and fields again once the sun had set. Liz showed immediate interest and suggested that they should ask her brother Bill if he would like to join them. "I know he doesn't talk, but he can point to things and indicate where he thinks something is amiss. " Smiling at Ian she went on "I bet my Bill knows as much about the countryside round here as you, and probably much more". Ian laughed and said "You're right there Liz, but don't tell our copper, or should I say ex-copper here."

Anne produced a detailed map of the area between the two villages and spread it out on the kitchen table. They all edged their chairs up to the table and began to carefully examine it. The two men retraced with their fingers the routes they had followed during their previous foray, and Liz, who had lived in the village all of her life, commented that they had certainly been thorough, and didn't appear to have missed any piece of ground. The two ladies then went in to the garden with Emily and the small dog to play and to enjoy the warmth of the sun. With no distractions the two men began to plot their course for the evening. They decided that they would begin at the Hawksmead end of the valley and work their way back towards Elwood. They would stay on the cricket ground side of the stream, traversing the slopes on that side. Their first port of call would be the farm of Jim Bailey.

Anne walked Liz home to her own house, and returned to cook a meal for the two soon to be explorers. Ian complimented Anne on her culinary skills having eagerly eaten the tasty meat and potato pie she had served up. "Did I detect rabbit in that tasty pie Mrs Evans?" asked Ian playfully. The apple and blackberry tart was consumed with equal relish. Now replete they set off on their evening adventure bidding farewell to Anne and Emily, but now accompanied by the eager Meg. The dog seemed to sense that tonight's walk would be something special, and she was particularly honoured to have two humans to guide. As they walked Ian asked his companion whether he thought that Bill would be able to help them in any way. Robert hesitated then said that maybe they could ask the old poacher to go with them later. He added that, for the time being Bill was so proud of his rejuvenated bike that he would have to have it surgically removed, before being asked to dismount to forage through the trees. Laughing, Ian informed him that the old man frequently rode the bike through the woods, slaloming through the trees to the surprise of the furry and feathered inhabitants therein.

Arriving at the Bailey farm Meg was enthusiastically and noisily greeted by the farm dogs there. Jim and Betty were busy collecting hens' eggs with the eager assistance of the twins. Alan was obviously in charge of the endeavour directing operations, and gently placing the precious harvest into the basket. He admonished one hen for producing a dirty egg, and another which pecked his little hand as he searched for further bounty. The farming pair were surprised to see the two men. They had heard of Robert's suspension, and his now employment on Dave Chalmers' farm, and were equally taken aback at his companion, a poacher who had had so many run-ins with the law. Briefly Robert told them what the purpose of their evening venture was, and how they hoped to bring some light on the two murders. He asked them once again about the strange lights and unusual noises they thought emanated from the vast forest. Jim repeated that they had only noticed these happenings on fairly rare occasions, and, looking at Ian, thought at the time that it was most probably poachers after pheasants. When Robert asked him from which area of the wood the noises came from, Betty replied that it was hard to pinpoint an exact spot as the trees tended to diffuse the sounds and the flickering lights. The only other information they could add was that, when they had heard the noises and seen the lights, it had always been on a rain-free night, and late evening or early night.

The two sleuth-hounds now bade farewell to the Bailey family and continued their search over the familiar ground they had already reconnoitred, the only difference being that, this time they had Meg as an additional seeker. The little dog was certainly taking her task very seriously, roaming all over the ground as they proceeded along the wooded slopes, overlooking the deep valley and the stream which sparkled in the fading light. As they entered a stand of deciduous trees which bordered the Bailey farm, they heard Meg yelping excitedly some distance in front of them. Quickening their steps, they discovered the indefatigable hound standing by an old tree stump, her tail wagging furiously. They both knew the reason for her interest, and Ian reached an arm into the stump to pull out a violently struggling rabbit. The poacher expertly killed the animal, and, taking his knife from his pocket, paunched it .Robert, in his turn, cut off a sturdy hazel sapling, and, with a cut in one leg of the rabbit to form a "v", slid the animal on to the pole and hefted it over his shoulder. He patted Meg to congratulate her on her hunting prowess and Ian remarked cheekily "We three make a good team, I think we should take up this poaching full-time."

The remainder of the hours of darkness passed without further alarms. Though they both had torches, it was hearing they were relying on for unusual sounds. While there was much rustling in the undergrowth and bats flittering about, only the mournful hooting of an owl disturbed the near silence of the woods. Seeing lights on in the Brisley home Robert thought that they should call in on the old couple to ask them about the odd goings on in the wood. The ladies welcomed the two men in and were only too eager to tell what they knew. Their observations were much the same as those of the Baileys, and, like them could not pinpoint the exact part of the forest from which the noises came. Thanking the ladies for their help, they left, but, as they walked down the path and were about to unlatch the gate, Maud came hurrying after them, flat-footed as ever, her feet at ten to two, clutching in her hand two bottles of Guinness! Waving goodbye they now continued their night-time walk. Ian, shining his torch on the bottle of brown liquid, said to his side-kick "Do you like Guinness Robert?" The look on his friend's face said it all, but with great courage the pair lifted the bottles and began to drink. After a couple of mouthfuls he admitted "Do you know I'm actually beginning to like this stuff". When it became obvious that the redoubtable Meg was beginning to flag, they decided to pack up and to return home. Within minutes of reaching the cottage, Meg was fast asleep on her cosy bed. Reviving mugs of cocoa and a welcome sit down to restore aching feet, Robert told Anne of their adventures and of Meg's heroics. Ian insisted on giving the rabbit to Anne who promised him a generous portion of the pie she would cook with it. Anne then suggested that he should stay the night as it was now very late, and the weary man gratefully accepted the offer.

CHAPTER TWENTY-THREE

Next morning, farming chores completed, Robert walked with Anne and Emily down to the village. After an essential visit to the bridge over the stream so that Emily could say hello to the ducks and the fishes that lived there, Anne went off to the shop where she would buy a newspaper, some groceries and perhaps some sweets for Emily. While they were in the shop Meg sat patiently on the pavement outside, just as she had been trained so to do. Robert then went to the pub for a meeting with the superintendent and the detectives. He was not surprised to see the prof, comfortably settled in an armchair, cuddling a glass of bitter in his large hand. He informed them that Ian would not be attending this morning as he had work to do. The super then asked him if anything extraordinary had happened on their trek through the countryside.

Robert spoke of their visit to the Bailey's farm, and their talking of the noises and lights emanating from somewhere in the forest, but were unable to pinpoint exactly where the activity was taking place. When he told them that the Brisley ladies had agreed with the Bailey's observations, and the gift of the Guinness, the prof asked "Where exactly do these two wonderful ladies live, I think I should call on them to thank them for their assistance. Did you say Guinness Robert, a favourite tipple of mine?" When the laughter had abated the superintendent asked Robert what he planned to do next. He said that he had heard nothing from the "spooks" in London, and for the moment at least the trail had gone cold. He said that they were all relying on him and Ian to find something on which they could focus their attention. They had no other possible leads to follow.

Robert answered that, this evening they intended to explore the other side of the valley, taking in the large forest, and that they would be taking the dog with them so that they could cover a larger area. Inspector Pengelly had been silent thus far, but he now icily remarked "We are wasting time now. I already had the prime suspect in the cells. I still think he had something to do with it. He had no alibis for the times of both of the killings, and nobody knows the country round here like him. This business of him not being able to talk, has he been fooling you? Let me question that daft sister of his. A good old-fashioned grilling would soon drag the truth out of her." Containing his anger Robert looked icily at Pengelly and replied "That man is a war hero. He has suffered grievously from his experiences in the trenches. You think he has been fooling everybody about his loss of speech. Do you really believe that he could have continued that charade for all these years since his return home? If you return that damaged old man to a prison cell, you will find your station besieged by the whole population of the area. "And", he asserted "I will be joining them, so you'd better get ready to suspend me again or put me in one of your cells."

Reg Weir hastily intervened by affirming that there was no intention of incarcerating old Bill. Pointing to the inspector he asked "if you think the old soldier is responsible for the murders, how do you account for the scarring and the partial writings on their backs, and what motive would he have for such callous behaviour?" Looking round the group he said that they should forget Silly Bill as a suspect, and concentrate elsewhere. Turning to Robert he said that he and Ian could hold the key to the mystery, if they could find some evidence that would advance the investigation. At that Pengelly rose from his chair and stormed from the room saying that he had urgent business elsewhere. At the door he turned briefly and gave a murderous look at Robert, causing the prof to declare "aren't we all on the same side here Inspector?". With Pengelly now gone the unpleasant atmosphere of the last few minutes went with him.

Superintendent Weir crisply explained exactly what he expected everyone to do this evening. He asked Robert to show him precisely where he and Ian would be stalking and at what time. He would give them a walkie-talkie so that they could keep in touch with him. He would remain at the pub with some other officers, and he would give these men permission to draw weapons in case of trouble. The people, he said, who had carried out these crimes were clearly prepared to use violence, and he told Robert to be careful. The prof asked if he too should remain at the Kings Arms should his expertise be required, and beamed happily when the Superintendent reluctantly agreed.

Sharing the milking duties with Dave that afternoon, Robert told the farmer of his plans for the evening, and the exploration of the forest. Dave offered him one of his dogs to help with the search, but Robert told him that his own dog Meg would go with them. He spoke of the incident with the rabbit on their latest jaunt, and Dave laughed saying "Trust Ian not to let an opportunity like that go begging." Robert told the farmer that he was seeing a different side to the young poacher, and he was beginning to respect his knowledge of nature and the lives of the creatures who inhabited the remote parts of the district. Dave looked unconvinced but accepted the (temporarily) ex-policeman's judgment. He said that, once the sun had gone down, he would be keeping a close watch on the wood, and, should the duo need any assistance, he stood ready to give it. Robert thanked his friend and, he hoped temporary, employer and gratefully accepted the stout ash stick which Dave gave him.

When Ian arrived at his home, Robert told him about the meeting at the pub, and of the strange behaviour of the fractious inspector. He showed him the communication device which he had been given and explained how it worked. He told him of the lack of progress in the case, and that the superintendent seemed to be relying on them to at least find some small clue which could carry them further forward. As the two men prepared to leave, both armed with thick staves, Anne begged them to be very careful in that dark and forbidding clump of trees. With Meg trotting proudly ahead they set off, heading first for the Hawksmead end of the wood. As the summer light faded, a brisk west wind began to blow and dark clouds raced menacingly across the evening sky with the threat of rain to come.

As they climbed the steep slope hundreds of rabbits scattered before them seeking the sanctuary of their warren, on the edge of the trees. Pigeons flew over their heads making their graceful way to their roosts for the night. Meg raced about hither and thither excited at all of this sudden activity. She almost caught one of the furry creatures as it disappeared down its burrow, and looked quizzically at Robert, ashamed at her failure to complete a successful hunt. Penetrating the wood by climbing over the formidable fencing, the two explorers, accompanied by their eager four legged buddy, began once more to systematically move purposefully along the sloping forest floor, with the dog ranging ahead of them. The going as ever was hard with the usual nettles and brambles tripping their feet and scratching legs and hands, despite their water-proof trousers and heavy coats. Both men stumbled from time to time as they stepped into rabbit and fox holes. Some noise was unavoidable, but they rarely spoke and that in a whisper.

After some twenty minutes of arduous walking, they decided to take a breather, sheltering under a great oak tree, whose summer raiment of leaves swaying now in the rising wind, offered them some respite from the increasingly heavy rain. Meg joined them and they all enjoyed a welcoming drink of water. A sudden crack of thunder and a brilliant streak of lightning brought drama to the scene, and they were reminded of the purpose of their night-time hike. Looking at the bedraggled farm worker/ policeman Ian remarked "this is the first time I've been out at night in the woods without having to look over my shoulder to avoid irate farmers or nosey coppers. Can you come with me every time I go hunting?" Robert smiled and said that, if he wasn't reinstated in the police force he might himself have to take up poaching to earn a living. He went on to say that, much as he enjoyed working for Dave Chalmers, the pay wasn't very good. Impulsively Ian shook his comrade's hand for long moments and said "I never thought I'd say this but I'm thoroughly enjoying working with one of the boys in blue." Clapping Ian on the shoulder Robert said "Let's get on then shall we", and they set off once more, and were soon approaching the centre of the forest where the trees were clustered ever more closely together, but at least the undergrowth was not quite so tangled. Looking down the slope Robert could just see the lights of Dave Chalmers' farm as the wind created momentary gaps in the foliage.

CHAPTER TWENTY-FOUR

They had progressed slowly perhaps a further two hundred yards when Meg, some distance ahead of them, began to bark excitedly. Her voice was clearly audible above the almost continuous peals of thunder, and the cracking of the lightning which momentarily illuminated the scene. Robert called the dog, but she refused to come back to him, continuing to yelp boisterously, and there was now alarm in her barking. The two men hurried towards her. From their previous visits to the forest they were aware of the huge hole in the floor of the wood. Dave Chalmers had mentioned this feature but had no explanation as to how it had been formed. He only thought that it was the home of badgers, but had never explored it.
Fighting their way through a particularly dense stretch of undergrowth, they emerged to find Meg prone on the ground and moaning in pain. As he bent down to administer to his pet, he inadvertently switched on his walkie-talkie so that their conversation would now be broadcast. Meg did not appear to be badly hurt, and she quickly struggled to her feet, wagging her tail at the sight of the two men. However they could not understand why she had created such a fuss, and how she had been hurt.

Their questions were quickly answered when they rose to be confronted by two large, knife-wielding men. They uttered something in a language which neither of them understood, and one of them raised his arms above his head, indicating that he demanded the same of his two captives. Robert warned the more excitable and aggressive Ian not to resist, but to do as they were ordered. When the wounded Meg ran at one of the men in an attempt to defend her master, she received another kick, which again rendered her unconscious. A furious Robert made to attack the dog beater but was stopped by a command in English to stand still. He turned to look at the newcomer and was astounded to see Inspector Pengelly, armed with a revolver which was unquestionably pointed at his head. A bemused Ian, staring at the policeman blurted "Copper, you're pointing that thing at the wrong man" indicating the two knife men. "I assure you, Englishman, I know exactly what I'm doing, and don't call me inspector. My name is Ivan Malenkov, and I am a Major in the Spetsnaz, a specialist organisation of the Soviet military." The two captives looked at each other in amazement, momentarily unable to take in what they were hearing. "What is this all about Major, or whoever you are, and who are these men?" As he said this Robert made a move towards his assailants, only to be threatened more forcibly by the gun and by the two large and menacing knives.

The two were now made to kneel on the wet ground and commanded to place their hands on their heads. A now recovering Meg painfully crawled to Robert, and sat by him, leaning on him for protection. Ignoring the menacing words of the men he now thought of as Russian, he bent down to comfort the little dog, surreptitiously laying the walkie-talkie on the ground beside her and scuffing some of last autumn's leaves over it, hoping by doing so he had not stopped their conversation being heard by the superintendent. Playing for time Robert asked the major "Where have these men come from, and how have they been hiding from us for so long?" The Russian major replied "I don't mind telling you as you won't live long enough to enjoy the knowledge. These brave comrades of mine have been living in the POW camp since the time when they arrived there together with the other Italian prisoners. You must realise that, as the war went on there was much confusion, and much changing of sides. Even that moron Hitler let Romanians, Czechs, Poles, Ukrainians and all sorts fight on the side of the Germans as the need for more soldiers became ever more desperate. It disgusts me to say that even some Russians were bribed or forced to join the wehrmarkt. When the Italian prisoners were shipped to this country of yours, my men were able to join them, so as to infiltrate themselves in to England. Only Kapitan Yuri Lermontov spoke Italian, and some English, and when they arrived at the camp, the authorities were only too glad for him to place his men in the hut where you found them. You will be meeting the Kapitan shortly, and I'm sure he will want to settle a score with you."

Thinking back over what Dicky Smith had told him of the disorganised arrival of the foreign soldiers to the camp, Robert could see how the Russians could have wormed their way in to the prison, and formed their own little clique in their own private billet, almost a sort of mini Russia. That the discipline in the facility had never apparently been really efficient was, to Dicky at least, a fact of life. However that tough regular soldier would himself have been amazed and humiliated to learn what had been going on inside the gates of the prison. There were, Robert knew, many such POW installations throughout the country, all, like this one, gradually emptying as the inmates were repatriated, and he wondered if they all operated in the same slapdash manner.

"Once your men were established within the walls of the camp, what did they intend to do, after all, you were our allies in the war. We fought together for four long years to defeat Hitler. Have you now suddenly become our enemies, or is this a part of some long-term plan?" Major Malenkov snorted, "You and your American friends could never really be brothers of the Soviet Union. We are socialists, and hate your capitalist way of life. Our beloved leader Yosif Stalin will not rest until the entire world is communist. There are groups of us all over your country. Our objective is to disrupt your institutions and your way of life."

It was rapidly becoming obvious to the two captives that the Russian officer, the erstwhile Inspector Pengelly, was enjoying telling them how they had so successfully infiltrated themselves in to the English countryside, and essentially made fools of the British military. Robert now wanted to find out more of the activities of the soviet soldiers, and of their plans. He did not doubt for one moment that he and Ian would be killed to prevent them from informing the authorities of what had been occurring in the POW camp. He felt that, even if he and Ian were killed, the walkie talkie would at least tell the listeners at the pub of the plans of the soviet leaders. Still playing for time, he asked how the fake Italian prisoners had managed to leave the camp without passing through the main gate. "You noticed how our hut backed on to some rough, almost impenetrable terrain. We simply dug a tunnel under the wire, and concealed the entrance and the exit so well that no-one was aware of its existence. The only guard we worried about was Corporal Smith, who seemed to be the only one who fulfilled his duties efficiently. Several times when he was sniffing around we thought of murdering him, but knew that an investigation might find us out." Robert was relieved to know that the likeable corporal had not been killed. Discovering how the Russians could free themselves from the confines of the camp, he asked where they went, and to what purpose. While he was talking he noticed that Ian was nudging ever more closely to one of their guards. He tried to warn him with a look not to attempt anything, but Ian suddenly launched himself at the man. He almost managed to grapple with him, but the other sentry was too quick and felled the poacher with a vicious blow to the head with the haft of his knife. With a moan Ian sank to the ground, and lay there temporarily at least unconscious.

When Robert went to help his friend he was halted by a waving of Malenkov's gun and a hissed "Leave him". Seeing Ian begin to stir, Robert, noting how the major was relishing being centre stage asked again where the Russians went on leaving the camp. Pointing to one of his compatriots he spoke to him in his own language and the man climbed gingerly in to the hole, and, between the roots of the vast beech tree which bordered the pit, he pulled aside a mass of foliage to reveal an opening big enough for a man to crawl through. It was so cleverly camouflaged that it was virtually invisible, unless someone stumbled upon it. From the newly opened aperture a light shone and there were sounds which Robert, as a former radio man, instantly recognised as communication signals. He now understood what the Brisley sisters and Jim Bailey had been hearing on occasions. It was evident that what had started as two particularly nasty murders, had now taken on a much more sinister turn. He hoped that the walkie-talkie was still working and that the police contingent in the pub could hear everything and be moving to go to the aid of Ian and Robert. The poacher, blood leaking from a nasty gash on his head, struggled to his feet, stood defiantly upright, and the look he gave his assailant was one of sheer malice.

"Do you like our little espionage nest Evans?" asked the major, evidently proud of what they had achieved. "You British had established hideouts like this all over your country so that in the event that the Nazis had invaded, men and women could conceal themselves in them and come out to ambush and harass the Germans. Our intelligence network, by nefarious means managed to discover the location of most of these, and some are now being used by Spetsnaz units like ours. It has all been beautifully planned, but I must admit that it was pure chance that our unit was sent to the POW camp in your village. We know that, when the camp is finally emptied, we shall have to find some other means of concealment and daily we await orders from Moscow. Now I'm getting tired of talking and we must end this. I do have some regret at having to execute you Evans, you are a brave man, and have been a worthy opponent." Robert now recalled what Dave Chalmers had told him of the army's activities in Oak Hill during the early part of the war, and could see how the Russian soldiers had made use of the facility.

CHAPTER TWENTY-FIVE

Putting his hand forward Robert shouted "Wait, surely you can tell us who the two young women were, and why were they murdered, after all that is why we have been searching the forest and questioning everybody to discover the truth. I assume that it was your people who were responsible for their deaths. Surely it was a mistake for you to call attention to this area by these brutal acts. Not quite as competent as you thought perhaps." The major angrily replied. "It was that idiot Lermontov . He was afraid that the girls would try to run away and betray us, but he should have disposed of them in such a way that their bodies would not be found". "But who were they"? Robert demanded, all the while looking for an opportunity to overcome the Russians.

"They were two Czech girls who, when the Germans invaded their country, fled to the east to the Soviet Union where they volunteered to join our forces. They, together with other nationalities, fought alongside our brave soldiers as we ejected the Nazis from our homeland. They were recruited into the spetsnaz not only because of their fighting skills, but for their skills in languages other than their own. They are both tall, well-built women, and, with short hair hidden beneath caps, and dressed like the rest of my men, it was easy to infiltrate them in to the prison." Confused Robert then asked "If they were such well-respected members of the group, why was it felt necessary to get rid of them, and why in those two particular woods?" Perhaps with a trace of regret in his voice the major explained, "They were becoming increasingly disenchanted with life in the camp. This was understandable, and all of my men felt much the same, but when the pair began to question the purpose of our presence in England, it was evident that they constituted a danger to our mission. It was necessary to keep a close guard on them, but, one Friday evening Eva managed to slip out of the hut. When her absence was noted several men were sent out after her intending to bring her back by force if necessary. It was Lermontov who found her. She refused point-blank to listen to his demands that she return to the camp, and so he despatched her with his knife. What he should have done of course was to bring her body back to the hut and conceal it there. Although we kept a closer watch on the other girl, Valentina, she too managed to overcome the idiot guarding her and she too legged it. Unfortunately for her she suffered the same fate as her compatriot."

"Was it the same killer?" asked Robert. "Of course" replied Malenkov, "Lermontov is rather skilled at that sort of thing, and had no compunction in executing her." "You make it sound rather noble, but to me it is simply murder, and, soldier or not, he should hang for it." Ian, who had been listening to the major now spoke "and he won't swing alone". As he said this he glared defiantly at the two knife-wielding guards. Robert tensed himself thinking that his friend was about to launch an attack on the Russian who had struck him. To divert attention from Ian, Robert asked the question which had bedevilled him and the detectives for so long in trying to make sense of the murders. "Why the horrible scarring on the girls' backs"?

"All spetsnatz officers and men have SSSR tattooed on their back to prove who they are. I realise now that our clumsy attempts to conceal the letters was not totally successful, but we thought that there would be nobody around here who could unravel the mystery of the scarring." They were all distracted by a burst of static coming from the now uncovered hideout. The major snarled an order to the Russian still in the entrance of the hideaway, who disappeared immediately into the depths of the cavern, and quickly came a sound that Robert recognised instantly as Morse code. Of course he could not decipher what was being transmitted and received, and he wished that his old headmaster could be here to help him. He leaned forward without receiving a warning from the Russians to see that the cave was quite substantial in size, and could easily accommodate a number of bodies. The major listened carefully to the communication, nodding and talking to his comrade. With the Russians now momentarily distracted, Ian glanced at Robert, and they both tensed ready to try to overcome their captors.

However a loud shout from somewhere below them towards the bottom of the wood caused everyone to look in that direction. Robert immediately recognised the voice of Dave Chalmers. The farmer, shotgun in hand, had been following the progress of the searching duo as they progressed through the trees. Despite the rain which was getting heavier by the minute, he could see the flickering of their torches, and walked along the edge of the wood keeping level with them. He had stopped when hearing Meg yelp, and the sound of raised voices, and he now called out to Robert to see that everything was alright. Malenkov ordered the man in the hole to switch off the communication equipment and to come out, concealing the entrance after him. He then ordered the other special services soldier to go and deal with Dave Chalmers. Fearing for his friend Robert yelled "It's OK Dave we're both fine. Why don't you go home and get out of this wind and rain."

Ian, feeling that now was the time to act if he and Robert were to survive the night, launched himself at the man who had hit him. Spurred into action Robert dived at the other knife man as he emerged from the cave. The major was, for the moment, unable to shoot for fear of hitting one of his own soldiers. Ian, weakened by his earlier injury, was slowly being overwhelmed by his stetsnaz opponent, but, just as Lermontov carefully aimed his revolver at the poacher, there was a high-pitched bellow of "TEN PAST TWO", and, weaving chaotically through the wet trees and undergrowth raced old Silly Bill, the light of battle in his eyes. Bell clanging, he now switched on his light and charged at the Russian Major, who stood no chance against the First World War veteran. Russian Special Forces soldier, Bill and bicycle fell together in a heap. As the two struggled furiously in the wet undergrowth, the revolver spilt from the major's hand. Using strength which belied his advancing years Bill managed to pin his opponent to the ground, and held him there yelling his war cry "TEN PAST TWO". As if to celebrate his victory there was a terrific crash of thunder.

Robert had quickly overcome his erstwhile captor, and rendered him hors de combat with a vicious karate chop to the throat. He then went to the aid of Ian, and together they subdued the Russian with Ian kneeling on his chest, and keeping him firmly under control. As he went to grab the major's gun he tripped on a tree root and fell heavily. Seeing that perhaps the tables were turned once more, Malenkov, with a supreme effort managed to push Bill off him and scrabbled though the debris on the forest floor to retrieve his revolver. Painfully rising to his feet after his stumble, Robert was looking down the barrel of a gun again. "It's over now Englishman" snarled the Russia taking careful aim at him. Ian could only look on in horror, unable to come to the aid of his friend. With his eyes shut, waiting for the end, Robert heard the bang, immediately followed by another one, but felt no pain. He opened his eyes to see the Russian major slowly toppling over to end up on the floor in an untidy heap, his chest a bloody mess. There was a stunned silence broken only by the sound of raindrops dripping through the foliage of the trees.

Dave Chalmers had realised that all was not well, with the two searchers, and had decided to clamber over the boundary fence and find out what was occurring. He had witnessed the fights between the Englishmen and the strangers, not knowing of course that they were Russian. He had also seen the epic ride through the trees of old Bill, and had marvelled at the way in which he had subdued the much younger strange man with a gun. Then, seeing Robert facing the weapon, and realising that the stranger intended to kill his friend, he had unhesitatingly levelled his shotgun at the would-be assassin, and fired both barrels killing him instantly. Badly shaken by the threat to his life and the stress and violence of the last minutes, Robert quickly recovered his equilibrium and firstly thanked Dave for saving his life. He then took the major's gun and told Ian to let his opponent up. He was relieved to see that Ian was OK but would have a sore head for some time yet. Meg too, frightened by the gunshots, was back to wagging her tail once again, and Robert was happy that Emily would soon be re-united with her little dog.

All of the men in that clearing in the wood needed time to absorb what had happened. The two Russians, both hurt, said nothing, probably as they had been taught, but in any case they appeared to speak no English. They were firmly under the control of Dave's, now reloaded shotgun, and the major's revolver in Robert's firm grip. He hoped that the superintendent and his men would have heard what of the dramatic happenings in the wood through the walkie talkie, still lying on the forest floor. Just as he began to lead everybody out of the trees, there was the sound of many bodies forcing their way through the wood. Wary of who the newcomers might be, Robert and Dave pointed their weapons in the direction of the threatening noise, while Ian waved a knife at the two prisoners. To Robert's relief soldiers in combat gear came bursting in to the clearing, some with sten guns, and others carrying Lee Enfield rifles. There were bellows in unmistakable English of "Hands in the air! Nobody move!" Then, walking sedately, like a galleon in full sail arrived Superintendent Reg Weir, like everybody else soaked through by the warm summer rain, but smiling in relief at seeing that Robert and his fellow warriors had everything under control.

At the guardroom of the camp Corporal Dicky Smith welcomed them with hot drinks, and turned on the heating to dry them all out until they could all get fresh clothing. An army medic dressed Ian's head wound, and also tended to the two Russians. Reg Weir explained that soldiers had entered the billet at the far end of the camp and had arrested the occupants who had surrendered without a fight. They had found the tunnel through which the Russians had managed to escape from the prison without being observed. Dicky tried to apologise for not having discovered the passage, but Reg said that the escape route had been so cunningly constructed that it could have fooled anyone. The one worry was that Lermontov, the murderer identified by Major Malenkov, had not been found, but that police and soldiers were scouring the area looking for him. He said that it was bizarre that they had inadvertently uncovered a dastardly plot to undermine the British way of life, while not being able to shackle the murderer of the two girls which had been the prime reason for the investigation. The superintendent thanked everybody, especially Bill for his dramatic rescue act which brought a wide smile to the old soldier's face, and a smart salute before setting off for home wheeling his slightly damaged bicycle. Robert promised him that he would see that repairs were effected as soon as possible. Shaking Dave Chalmers' hand Reg Weir expressed his profound thanks to the farmer for his timely intervention in the stand-off in the woods, and assured him that he would be helping out with the milking as soon as he could. Then, with a broad grin on his craggy features he enquired "I assume you've got a licence for that gun of yours?" There was laughter all round as they departed to go their separate ways. As they left the superintendent told them that he wanted them all to come to the Kings Arms the next morning so that he could sum up the troubling events of the last few weeks.

CHAPTER TWENTY-SIX

It wasn't until he got home that the stress of the events of the night in the forest caught up with Robert. Anne had been waiting up for him and, as they embraced he could not stop trembling and was close to tears. Out of his wet clothing and now warm and dry once again, he told her how he and Ian had been confronted by men who he now knew were Russian soldiers. She was shocked when he told her that the policeman they thought of as a police inspector was, in reality, a major in a special soviet intelligence unit. He did not go into details of the violence, not wanting to upset her, but told her how old Bill and then Dave Chalmers had come to their rescue. Emily had been woken by her dad's talking and came to hug him and her mum, thankfully unaware of how close he had come to being badly hurt or even killed. The little girl fussed over Meg too. The dog had completely recovered from her hurts, and Robert had no intention of telling Emily of the bad treatment she had received at the hands of the nasty men.

Robert, Anne and Emily then retired to the big bed to spend what was left of the night cosily together. Silently Meg crept in to the bedroom and craftily climbed on to the foot of the bed and curled up to sleep. Soon all were peacefully asleep and only the gentle whimpering of the little dog was to be heard.

When he arrived at the King's Arms Robert was not at all surprised to find Doctor Buchanan firmly ensconced in a comfortable armchair in the room at the pub which they all thought of as their conference room. The doc greeted him warmly, arms crossed over his ample belly. In front of him on the table was the inevitable glass of ale, half empty. The two were quickly joined by Superintendent Weir, and the two detectives Malcolm Alvey and Trevor Bailey. Ian then arrived sporting a bandage around his head. He brushed off their concerns about his injury and said that he was fine, but, laughingly he informed Reg Weir that he would be claiming substantial damages from the police for his hurt. Clapping the poacher on the shoulder, Weir said that explanations were now called for, loose ends to be tied up. They all nodded in agreement.

"Before you begin" broke in the doc, pointing to his now empty glass. Obediently landlord Stan picked up the glass and made off for the bar, asking as he went whether anybody else required sustenance. Only Ian answered in the affirmative saying that the nurse had recommended alcohol to aid his convalescence. "A man after my own heart" breathed the doc.

From his briefcase Reg Weir produced a sheaf of papers and, putting on a pair of horn-rimmed spectacles began to talk. "First of all," he said, "let's clear up the mystery of Inspector Pengelly aka Major Malenkov. His papers have been closely scrutinised and found to be excellent forgeries. It's obvious now that he chose to embed himself in the local police station so that he could be near his compatriots at the POW camp. By the way", he went on, looking at Robert "he of course had no authority to suspend you. You are once again a member of the constabulary, and indeed, I have decided to promote you to sergeant as of today." Robert gratefully accepted the congratulations of the others, and, predictably the doc thought that the good news must be properly celebrated with something of an alcoholic nature. Stan, happy to boost his finances even further quickly set off for the bar ready to set the till into action. The super now turned to Ian "As for you, you young scallywag, I've recommended an award for you, Dave Chalmers and old Bill for your assistance in helping us, and for putting yourselves in danger without a thought for your own safety. Robert was delighted for his friends while Ian looked embarrassed. He had spent much of his life in trouble and this praise was something completely new to him. Looking at Robert he chuckled "Now you're a sergeant, you will be too important to bother about trivial things like poaching won't you?"

The superintendent now went on to discuss the camp. He had hoped to have Corporal Smith here but Dicky was busy doing an accurate roll-call of the remaining prisoners, keenly aware of the sloppiness of the past. "The administration of the camp has been a complete mess from the very moment that the prisoners first arrived. It appears that no true account of the numbers brought in was ever made. While this may have been understandable owing to the general chaos of war, a simple headcount, and identification of each prisoner should have been carried out. There will certainly be an investigation as to how a soviet cell was allowed to install itself within the confines of a British POW facility. I understand that Intelligence is strenuously looking at all the other POW camps dotted about throughout the country. They will also be searching the many boltholes we set up to harass the Germans should they have invaded. The Russians in the local camp will be interrogated by our security men, but we know that they will say nothing, as they are trained to do. Ultimately they will be returned to the Soviet Union, since they are soldiers of that country, and, apart from espionage, have committed no crimes here. We believe that the gulag awaits them on their return to their own country, and they will find conditions there much less comfortable than the camp here . Our Prime Minister intends to severely censure the Soviet authorities for allowing their agents to attempt to sabotage the governance of Great Britain."

Reg paused momentarily while he consulted the papers in front of him. "As we all know this spying bit came to light because of the murder of the two young women in the woods. Malenkov told you that their names were Eva and Valentina and that they were of Czech nationality. We have asked the Czech authorities for help in finding out their proper names, but, at the moment they hold out little possibility of discovering this as their country, like most of Europe, is still trying bring order to their society, encumbered by the many refugees milling about, themselves looking for a home and relatives. "Robert broke in now and asked when the bodies of the girls could be released for burial. He said that he would ask Reverend Harris if they could be buried in the churchyard of St. Michaels. He was certain that the parishioners would not object to this. Reg Weir made no objection to this, and the doc irreverently enquired if the wake would be held in the Kings Arms.

It was Ian who asked the question which had been troubling them all for some time now "Who," he asked "bought the forest from Mr. Chalmers?" "Good question," replied Weir, "We honestly don't know. The purchase was done through some obscure company based somewhere in the Caribbean. Of course we now know the real reason for buying the wood, and the Soviet Union was really behind it. It'll probably be up for sale shortly. Perhaps Dave Chalmers might be interested in buying it back .The bolthole in the forest has been thoroughly searched, and the communication equipment taken away for examination. The hole will now be filled in."

Shaking hands all round Superintendent Reg Weir now rose to leave signalling that the meeting was at an end. He thanked everybody once again for their support, and promised that, when he had finished all the usual paperwork attached to the case, he would return to the village to milk some cows and enjoy a pint or two in the pub. Walking somewhat unsteadily out of the room Doctor Buchanan turned and questioned "Only a pint or two Reg?"

Leaving Ian to enjoy a game of darts in the pub, Robert set off for home. He was almost a happy man, happy at his unexpected promotion, and the praise that his actions, and the actions of Ian, Dave and Bill had received from the superintendent, but still deeply concerned that the brute who had murdered two girls was still at large. Until he was behind bars he would remain a potential threat to the people of the village.

CHAPTER TWENTY-SEVEN

As he approached his cottage Robert saw that the garden gate was wide open. This was unusual as they didn't want Meg running out into the lane to be run over by one of the few vehicles which used the road. Thoughtfully he closed the gate and walked up to the door, where he called out loudly to let Anne know that he was back, and opened it. Entering the kitchen he was confronted by the worst of all nightmares. Standing in the middle of the room was his beloved wife, and behind her with a large knife pressed against her throat was Kapitan Yuri Lermontov, a look of hatred on his face. In the corner of the room, in the dog's bed crouched a terrified Emily clutching her little dog. Robert knew that any hostile move on his part would probably lead to Anne's death, and so he stood stock still, calmly looking for a way to overcome the murderous Russian. Lermontov spoke in his fractured English "Move and she is dead policeman, and then I kill your daughter and the dog as well". In measured tones Robert answered "What must I do to prevent that Captain? I know that you don't really want to kill anybody." "You are forgetting that I have already executed two young women just like this one. Now you do exactly as I tell you. You will order up a police car, and you will drive all of us to a place where I know that friends of mine will be waiting."

Anne was unable to move with the threat of the knife, but there was no fear in her eyes, only determination as she looked at her husband. When Emily whispered "Mummy, who is this nasty man, will he hurt us?" She replied "It's alright darling, daddy's here now. " Robert had never been so proud of his wife, and the firm look he gave her was saying "Courage darling, we'll get through this together." Again speaking calmly Robert said that he would need to telephone to get a car, and Lermontov motioned him towards the phone snarling "No tricks Evans". He had now made a fatal error for he had used the hand which held the knife to point to the phone. The pressure on her throat now eased, Anne bit hard on the Russian's wrist causing him to yell out and to loosen his grip on his captive. With two short steps Robert plunged forward and punched Lermontov hard in the face putting all of his considerable strength and anger into the blow. The Russian fell to the floor, the knife falling from his hand, and Anne rushed to Emily who held her arms out to her dear mother. Robert picked up the knife, gave it to Anne and told her to run outside and go to the village for help. He then turned his attention to the man who had already murdered two people and had now threatened his own family in his own home.

The Russian spetsnaz soldier rose groggily to his feet, still partly dazed by the savage punch he had received. As he looked at the large policeman he felt despair. He had already felt the power of this man twice now, and realised that he would be beaten unless he could find another weapon. He staggered round the kitchen seeking a knife or anything he could use as a weapon. Implacably Robert pursued him raining blows on him. His weapons were his fist and the power which fuelled his anger. Left and right handed blows, delivered with accuracy and venom, reduced the Russian to helplessness. His face a mass of blood, nose and jaw broken and teeth missing, and ribs probably fractured, he collapsed on to the kitchen floor, moaning and half unconscious. Robert bent over him and growled, "This is for the two poor little women you massacred, for the anxiety you have caused to my people in the village, and mostly for endangering my precious family. I hope you hang, not because your politics are different from mine, but because you are a foul, uncaring thug, and the world will be well rid of you." He called through to Anne to tell her that he was ok, and that they were safe. With tears in her eyes she smiled at Robert and laid down the poker which she had picked up help him should it be needed. She had phoned the police for help and knew that they would be there soon.

Sirens echoed through the valley as police cars raced along the lane to the cottage. Armed officers rushed in and quickly handcuffed Lermontov. Examining the Russian's face one of the policemen asked Robert "Did you do this? What did you hit him with? Remind me not to fall out with you" Nursing his bruised knuckles he smiled and turned to hug Anne and Emily as they now came in to the room, relief on their faces when they saw that their man was unharmed. Soon all of the visitors, some welcome, and one not so, had gone. Anne suggested that a walk to the village and the stream was called for, and Emily, Meg as ever at her side, happily ran to her most favourite place in the whole world to wonder at the sparkling, gently meandering water with the little fishes swimming elegantly along. Hand in hand Emily's mum and dad watched their daughter with love and pride in their faces. They both knew that the events of that awful afternoon would linger long in their memory, but they would find the strength to put it behind them and look forward to a bright future. Their love for each other had never been stronger.

If they expected a peaceful evening they were sorely mistaken as a stream of friends and acquaintances, having somehow heard of the dramatic goings on at the Evans' home, came to see that all was well, and that nobody had been hurt. A veritable mountain of flowers for Anne, toys for Emily and treats for Meg were brought. For Robert there were congratulations on his re-instatement into the police force, and on his promotion to the rank of sergeant. The Brisley sisters were concerned that he might now be assigned to another station, but he was able to promise them that he would continue to be their local bobby. In return they promised him that there would always be a Guinness for him whenever he visited them. "That nice Doctor Buchanan likes our Guinness as well" said Maud. Reg Weir also came apologising that they had not been able to apprehend Lermontov before his assault on Robert and his family. When Ian arrived on his motorbike, he was rewarded with a big hug from Anne which caused the young man to blush furiously. At last they were alone once again. After an evening spent cuddled together on the wide sofa, with Meg on Emily's lap, they retired to bed, all huddled close together, while outside a bright moon shone in a near cloudless sky, and the vast array of stars twinkled happily, watching over them.

CHAPTER TWENTY-EIGHT

It had to end where it had all started, and it was ironic that the two teams contesting the cricket match today were those that had taken the field on that fateful day earlier in the summer. It was a lovely warm Sunday when Robert, accompanied by his wife, daughter and faithful spaniel set off from their cottage to walk the short distance to the ground. As they approached the field Robert could see how everyone had taken great pains to make everything look spick and span. The wicket was tightly mown and the outfield too was closely cut. A lick of paint made the pavilion gleam in the sunlight and the Union Jack fluttered proudly from the flagpole atop the pavilion. The creases on the wicket were sharply delineated, and he noted that the stumps, already in place, had a look of newness about them.

Robert thought that there might be extra interest in the game today since the village had received much coverage in the local and national press. The club secretary had proudly announced that he had received a letter from Lords wishing the club well, and had sent a bat signed by all of the members of the MCC team. Anticipating a larger audience than usual, chairs and benches had been requisitioned from the village hall, and most were already occupied. Young girls were going round with raffle tickets to sell to boost the finances of the club. The three veterans were already installed in their deckchairs, and today, were sporting their wartime medals, and only squabbling very gently over which were more valuable and more deserved than the others. In the pavilion there was a veritable feast of sandwiches, pasties, buns and cakes baked lovingly by the wives of the cricketers. To the side of the pavilion, in his little hutch, scorer Gerald was seated, today unusually wearing a smart three-piece suit and a bright yellow tie. His unruly locks were tightly treacled down, and his array of multi-coloured pencils sat ready to be deployed.

Anne and Emily sat down on the veranda of the pavilion, and they both gave Robert sloppy kisses, and whispered good luck as their champion walked to the home dressing room. As he entered it there was a spontaneous round of applause from his teammates. The skipper congratulated him on his promotion and said "I know it's going to be a warm day, but we felt that you might like to put this on today". He then presented the embarrassed Robert with a handsome white pullover, apparently knitted by old Bill's sister Liz. Examining the exquisite gift he saw that, on both sleeves was sewn the chevrons of a police sergeant! Robert's opening partner Brian said that he must now go out and score a ton to justify the insignia proudly displayed on his arms.

As the clock on the church spire chimed two, the umpires, their white coats shining white, made their stately way to the wicket. Placing the bails on the stumps, they then checked that all was ready to let the contest begin. The visitors from Hawksmead, led by Ian Friend, captain for the day, made their way to the centre, and the fielders deployed to their respective positions. They were respectfully received by the spectators with polite applause, but when Robert and Brian emerged from the pavilion there were cheers, something rarely heard on cricket grounds. The fielding team also clapped the batsmen to the wicket, smiling at the badges on Robert's sleeves. It was déjà vu with Ian opening the bowling and Robert facing the first delivery. "Leg stump" called Robert to the umpire, and, after a few wiggles of his bat he marked the crease and looked round the field. He noticed that there were three slips and a gulley, and thought "Ian's certainly going to be quick today". He also noted that all of the fielders were close to the wicket with no third man, long on or long off. It was assuredly an attacking field.

Ian now marked out his run-up, some five yards longer than usual, and did some loosening up exercises. Everyone, players and spectators alike, were tensed, waiting to see what would happen when Ian fired his first fast delivery. Then a strange thing happened. As the umpire called "Play, all of the fielding side raced off to the far end of the field heading for the lane and the wood where the first young lady had been found. They were followed, at a much more sedate pace by the two umpires. Reaching the boundary fence they all held their hands out in a catching position. Ian, a broad grin all over his face, roared up to the wicket and bowled at an equally smiling Robert. It was a tennis ball which left the bowler's hand and was despatched with some power to the square-leg boundary to be easily caught one-handed by Superintendent Weir, come to enjoy an afternoon's cricket.

Now the serious business of the cricket match began. As ever both sides would play hard to gain the advantage over their opponents. Ian, and his fellow bowlers strove with every sinew to remove obstinate batsmen and the fielders, wanting to back up the bowlers, moved purposefully about the field. The appeals were vociferous and decisions accepted, some reluctantly, but never queried. Both Robert and Ian reached fifty, but after that wickets fell, and the final score was not a winning one. However, when the Hawksmead side batted, they fared little better, and perhaps, as if it was ordained, the match ended in a tie.

As Robert walked a little wearily along the lane to his home after the game, he felt happier than he had for some time now. The horrors of the past few weeks were now behind him. The vile murderer was safely behind bars, and a dangerous espionage ring had been uncovered. More importantly he had cemented new friendships with some locals who had, until now, been acquaintances rather than friends. Above all he could now call Ian Friend, his former nemesis, someone on whom he could rely (but he didn't really expect him to stop his poaching activities).

Reaching his garden gate, he paused and looked down the valley at the houses and cottages, the church and Emily's stream, at the cattle and sheep grazing peacefully in the meadows. And he looked up to the forest, no longer sinister, but serene with the trees glowing a golden colour in the rays of the retiring sun. The door of his cottage opened and there stood his wife Anne, with his treasured daughter Emily, Meg at her side. Stretching her arms towards him Anne breathed "Welcome home darling sarge!" Just then there was the tinkling of a bicycle bell and a loud TEN PAST TWO and old Bill raced past, grinning from ear to ear, and Sergeant Evans thought "all's well with the world once again".

Printed in Great Britain
by Amazon